Dedicated to
Mary Luallen,
who brings joy to everyone she knows.

Ms Mia

and

Murder

at the

Spinel Reef Resort

Jennifer Branch

Spinel Reef Resort

1

Arrivals

Buck hauled the last of Mia's luggage onto his boat. "Sure that's all you're bringing?"

The matching aluminum cases filled the stern of the motorboat, piled on every horizontal surface. The two captain's chairs barely crested above the sea of shiny luggage.

"I didn't think I'd need much for a beach trip," Mia replied seriously, completely undaunted by his teasing. "Caribbean clothing is much lighter than a cold weather wardrobe."

"Lighter, huh?" Buck stowed the last case neatly away below. "I'd hate to keep up with your bags when you travel anywhere cold."

"They generally get to me eventually." She lovingly stroked the smoothly varnished gold of the wood.

"Your boat is gorgeous, Buck. How long have you had her?"

Buck thumped the gleaming instrument panel proudly. "1957 Chris Craft 32 Vintage Express Cruiser. I spent the past year rebuilding her from the ground up."

"She was certainly worth the effort." Mia admired the sleek lines of the boat. "They don't build them this beautifully anymore."

"It gave me something to do." Buck swiped at his close cropped silver hair with one hand, clenching the wheel with tightly white knuckles. "I tell you, Mia, after Sarah died, I didn't know what I was going to do with my life. We'd always planned everything together. All our retirement plans were us, together. Not me on my own."

"Sarah was very special, Buck." Mia squinted out at the ocean, her eyes tearing up behind her oversized round sunglasses. "It's hard to keep going sometimes, I know. But it's what she would have wanted."

He gestured at the wide blue sea with a broad sweep of his muscular, tanned hand. "Setting me up running dive operations and the reef restoration really gave me a purpose. Something to do every morning, a reason to get up. And this little lady, well, she's filled my evenings." He patted the gleaming wood and shot a quick glance at her. "Anyway, thanks." He awkwardly cleared his throat and blinked rapidly, retreating behind his sunglasses.

"It was what Leo and Sarah would have wanted." Her warm pink lips curved into a sudden smile. "It's not like having an ex Navy Seal running the dive center is exactly bad for business, Mr. Master Chief."

He barked a laugh and swiped at his silver hair again.

"And I had to have someone I could trust with the reef restoration. I can't wait to hear all about it."

"When we dive, you won't believe the progress made since you were here last year. I can't believe how those tiny coral fragments have taken off, and I help measure the things. And the fish, all the colors of the rainbow. New species appear all the time. It's amazing to see it developing," he told her.

"I can't wait to see." Mia and her husband, Leo, had often gone on dive trips with Buck, Leo's childhood friend, and Sarah, Buck's wife. Whenever they'd taken on a hotel with interesting dive possibilities, they'd invited the other couple to join them on the adventures and brainstorm ideas. The reef restoration at the Spinel Reef Resort was a cherished project of Mia's. Growing a coral garden, where one had been destroyed a century ago by unwise dredging, was a dream come true. She couldn't wait to dive and see the changes.

She gazed out at the turquoise water surrounding her, smiling with pleasure. The boat trip to the hotel's island was always exciting, especially when she could see nothing but blue sea and sky as far as the horizon in all directions. She relaxed into the steady roar of the engine and feel of the wind on her face, feeling stress leaving her body.

"Mia?" Buck broke into her reverie. "Mia, Mark was telling me you'd been a little busy lately and really needed a break. And something about finding dead bodies? What's that?" His brow furrowed into marked tanned creases.

She focused on him, crossing her legs and carefully positioning them to an elegant angle, neatly propped up on her largest suitcase. Mark, her stepson and the Spinel Resorts CEO, must have told Buck to check up on her. She was glad she had such an attentive son, but could have done without his constant, nagging concern. "Buck, it's nothing to worry about. There were a few murders at hotels while I stayed there. They were all cleared up and the police arrested the murderers. So there's absolutely nothing to worry about. It's all in the past." She carefully didn't mention that she'd helped clear the murders up—and risked her life doing so.

"Mark said he thought you needed a good long break—you'd been overdoing it." Speaking a little awkwardly and determinedly focusing on the sea ahead, he added, "Lots of gossip between hotels, you know."

"Don't I know it," Mia sighed. "A nice break from murder and mayhem sounds nice, Buck. I'm completely on vacation for this trip—I know you all have everything under control at this hotel, unlike Arizona." She shuddered a little at the memory, "That was a complete mess." She'd spent the past few months getting the Spinel Desert Sunrise Resort up to Spinel standards. "Really, I could do with a relaxing break. Dive trips to the reef, long walks on the beach, lovely Caribbean cuisine and the spa all sound wonderful right now."

He nodded sharply. "That's what you'll get, then."

A loud noise broke into the sound of the engine and waves whipped up, misting her in froth as a helicopter flew low overhead. Mia patted her hair down, resettling it into its accustomed waves.

Buck nodded at it and whistled. "Nice, a Sikorsky S-76. That must be Skip what's his name. You know, the Blare whiz kid. Evie was pulling out the red carpet for him."

"Skip Wilson?" Mia asked. "I would have thought he'd rent his own island, not stay at a hotel." Skip Wilson, she knew, had taken the social media world by storm. His video sharing app bestowed instant fame or condemned users to instant obscurity. She hadn't used it yet, but her daughter was always uploading something and chattering about likes. Mia had seen the headlines about Skip Wilson in the news, however. Her mouth twisted in a tight moue, "Especially not one of our hotels. They're a bit family oriented and quiet for his crowd."

Buck shrugged. "Maybe he likes being around people. He does do social media, after all, so he must like being around people."

"Well, he's certainly not going to have the kind of parties he's used to on my island," Mia said tartly. "He'd better plan on a relatively quiet vacation."

Buck shrugged again, completely confident in being able to handle anything that happened on the island. "Maybe that's what he wants this week."

As they approached the island, a long gray dock stretched out to meet them, bobbing on the water with a neat hut perched at the end. Buck pointed out to it as they passed. "The reef and the new dock. Looks like a dive party is out there now." A bright red dive flag bobbed proud of the waves, warning of those below the surface.

Buoys warned against boats approaching the young reef. Buck swung his Chris Craft around sharply, cut the motor, smartly easing the boat into her slip in the little marina.

Mia always loved her first sight of the island, shining bright under the deep blue sky. Low white buildings ringed with breezy porches complemented the long expanse of gleaming white beach, broken only by the rich greens of palm trees against the sky.

Buck stepped onto the dock and held out his hand. "Here you are, milady." He grinned at her. "I'll send someone down for that mountain of luggage. Once was enough." He rubbed his muscular tan arm with a mock grimace, then squinted out at the horizon. "Looks like the ferry's arriving. We always beat 'em, though. Can't keep up with my girl here." He patted his boat.

The large boat, ringed with eager guests around the railings, pulled up to the end of the dock. Mia noticed several children physically restrained by loving hands from leaping over the side, buzzing with eagerness. A man, smartly dressed in creased white shorts and a turquoise blue polo shirt emblazoned with the hotel logo, tied the dock line off, then began helping people disembark with a welcoming smile and steady arm. Mia grinned as he said for the tenth time to a tourist struggling to unload their large suitcase and completely blocking the gangway to the dock, "No, no, sir, we will send a bell boy for the baggage. Please, sir, we'll handle it." She wondered how many heavy suitcases had slipped from tourists' hands into the ocean as they navigated from the bobbing boat to the dock. Much better to collect the bags and deliver them safely to guest's rooms. Several young men with full carts lined the dock's end, accompanied by a flock of departing guests shepherding their luggage.

Mia and Buck allowed themselves to fall a little behind the straggling group heading to the hotel. They kept to the side of the dock so departing guests, sunburnt and chattering about return plans, could board the ferry. It would be easier for Mia to greet her friends on the resort team after the other guests were checked in.

A line of uniformed employees trotted out to the helicopter pad to greet the VIP arrival with appropriate fanfare, if not an actual red carpet. A beefy young man with a burgeoning paunch and muscular arms held them back from the helipad, obviously checking those approaching before letting them anywhere near the arrivals. He must be the security guard, Mia decided, as a young man, thin shoulders hunched against any sudden onslaught, disembarked. Skip Wilson was a lot thinner and less confident looking than she'd seen in his press conferences. His tattered Nirvana t-shirt and faded jeans were not prepossessing. Light brown hair was blown straight up by the wind like a dandelion, revealing an incipient bald spot, and his shoulders curved protectively around the laptop bag he carried with both hands. Maybe he did just need a quiet vacation, Mia thought. Skip Wilson didn't look like he was in any kind of shape for wild parties.

"Mia!" a warm voice called out and Evie Ferguson, the hotel manager, rushed to her with a broad grin. "I'm so glad you're here!" She hugged Mia enthusiastically, her round cheeks just brushing Mia's.

"It's been forever since your last stay." She nodded at the helicopter and ferry crowd, "It's a bit crazy at the moment, but I can't wait to catch up." Her eyes darted back as a private boat swung into the marina. She smoothed her crown of intricately woven braids that increased her apparent height by at least three inches. "There's another arrival. Always guests come all at once."

"Never a dull moment at a hotel," Mia smiled at her friend, tiny lines crinkling around her bright blue eyes. "I'm here for a nice long vacation, so I'll see you when you have a chance to chat."

"I can't wait to catch you up with all we've been doing," Evie enthused with a smile, doe brown eyes bright. "And I'd love your advice on a few things."

Buck told Evie firmly, "Vacation, remember. Mia's here for a break."

"Oh, yes. Yes, of course," Evie looked a little flustered, straightening her loose floral dress around her plump figure. "You'll have a completely relaxing vacation, Mia. Don't you worry about a thing. Not a single thing. We'll take care of you right." She nodded firmly, lips slightly pursed. Then, her eyes flickered over at the crowd around the helicopter. "I'd better go check the VIP in. From what I've heard, he just loves the extra attention." She rolled her eyes expressively. Giving Mia a cheerful wink, she added, "Don't worry, your cottage is on the other side from Mr. Wilson's. I've heard all about those parties of his." She hugged Mia one more time and hurried to join the celebrity entourage.

A voice called, "Buck!" and the concierge, Sandra Rolle, waved her hand, motioning him over. An athletic, tanned group surrounded her, festooned in the latest dive gear, obviously itching to meet their renowned dive master.

"See you later, Mia," he told her and strode over to the group. She watched as he pointed to the dive dock, then started walking down with the dive group, enthusiastically gesturing at the clear blue water. A woman peered over the side and squealed excitedly; the guests clustering around her find. Buck stood over them, beaming as proudly as if he'd called the fish over himself.

The island was a good fit for Buck, Mia decided with a smile. She looked at the large crowd waiting to check in, then chose an inviting rocking chair overlooking the beach and dock. New arrivals surveyed the beach and hotel enthusiastically, calling out interesting finds and exclaiming at the beauty of the island. A departing guest, floppy straw hat clutched in one hand while the other waved frantically, ran down the marina dock, barely making it onto the ferry as it departed, ably assisted by a deck hand swinging her onto the deck with a white toothed grin. He closed the railing chain with an air of finality.

A caravan of luggage carts trundled back into the hotel, shepherded by smiling young men in crisp uniforms. Guests hurried to point out their bags and room numbers, and the fleet separated to the various rooms. She saw her own shiny aluminum stack—taking up an entire cart on its own—presumably en route to her cottage. She wondered which one Evie had chosen for her this trip.

From what Mia remembered, the majority of Spinel Reef Resort's guests reshuffled about once a week. Most people stayed one week, arriving on Saturday and departing the next Saturday. There were several all-inclusive packages the hotel offered, and most guests took advantage of the multiple dive options. There were, of course, always a few guests who stayed only through a long weekend, unable to leave their normal routine for any longer. Since the Bahamas was a relatively easy getaway from the eastern United States, the hotel was usually booked solid, even if the only time it actually felt full was during the flurry of Saturday departures and arrivals. A few retired snowbird guests stayed for most of the winter as well, glad to get away from their icy homes for a few months without dealing with the problems of owning a house in a foreign country.

She spotted a self-important older man in well worn dive gear, carrying an officious clipboard, pushing his way through the newcomers like an aging salmon swimming upstream. A gawky young man trailed behind him, lugging a heavy bag. Spinel Reef offered a residency program to scientists or graduate students every season. The current incumbents, Dr. Sebastian Barbeau and his grad student, were documenting the reef restoration project, with a focus on the timing of the different species' arrivals. She looked forward to discussing his studies with him.

A tall glass, frosted with condensation, was adroitly placed at her elbow. Looking up, she saw the smiling face of George, the headwaiter. "George!" She quickly stood up and hugged him in greeting.

"It's been a while since you were with us, Ms. Mia," he beamed in welcome. "I brought you a glass of switcha, to get you started."

"Thanks, George," she sipped the tart refreshing drink, made from key limes. "That is perfection. I missed the island."

"Glad you're back with us," he hurried off to fill the new guests' drink orders, still beaming cheerfully as he fielded orders with easy efficiency.

"Ms. Mia!" Sandra Rolle, the concierge, hurried over and gave her a hug. "So good to see you! You're all set up at the Yellow Bells Cottage; here's your key." She looked back at her beleaguered assistant manning the long line at the desk and hugged Mia one more time. "Gotta go!" Her crisp white skirt swished as she returned to her guests. Sandra's bold orange and turquoise headscarf coordinated perfectly with her uniform polo shirt and the white classic tennis shoes were just right for long days on her feet. Some days, Mia mused, it would be nice to just wrap a headscarf around her hair and get going. No more bad hair days. Not that she ever allowed her hair to have those. She patted her smooth ash blonde locks, elegantly in place.

Sipping her cold glass of switcha with pleasure, she was in no hurry to leave the stunning beach view. The crowd had started clustering into groups, some eager to get their swimsuits on and splash in the waves, some content to drink tall, frosty concoctions and admire the scenery. Now that she had her key, she could escape to her cottage haven any time she wanted, but she enjoyed watching the hectic scurrying of the new arrivals. It was nice being at a resort that she didn't need to fix.

A middle aged woman juggling several heavy bags trudged up the path from the marina. She looked hot and tired, her sweaty blond hair showing dark roots in furrowed rows of scraped back hair trapped in a stringy ponytail.

Mia called out, "One of the hospitality team would be happy to take that to your room for you." She caught one of the young men's eyes and motioned to him. He whisked the bags onto his cart and stood politely waiting for directions.

The woman smiled at her. "Thanks. Two carryons is my handling limit. The duffle with my husband's dive stuff put it over the top." She scowled. "And," she made a face, "he ditched me to go check out that dive dock you're supposed to have." She shook her head disgustedly, "Some second honeymoon this is." Stretching out sore muscles, she pointed to a distant figure far out on the beach, her thin mouth pursed like she'd sucked a lemon. "Just look at him."

"I'm sure he's just excited," Mia commiserated. "Why don't you check in and relax for a bit?" She added, "Sometimes it takes a day for vacation mode to kick in."

The woman barked a laugh and wiped beads of sweat off her brow. "As if he ever relaxes." She grimaced and shook her head. "I'm going to enjoy myself, anyway. Spa treatments, here I come."

"That's the spirit," Mia agreed. "Relax, then you can have some fun together."

The woman left for the lobby, motioning to the bell boy to follow.

Sipping her drink, Mia enjoyed the gentle breeze from the porch fans hanging from the white rafters. It was a lovely late afternoon, sun slowly lengthening the violet shadows. A few guests started up a game of beach volleyball. None of them were very good, but they had fun just getting the ball over the net. They spent more time running to keep it out of the sea than with it in the air. Cries of "Ball" and happy laughter melded with the steady sound of ocean waves against the shore.

Couples walked hand in hand down the white sands, leaning close and embracing, their feet in the ocean. A large pasty white man in brightly flowered swimming trunks lumbered into the waves, grinning in delight as he bobbed, suddenly weightless in the clear turquoise water. Children laughed as they wiggled their toes in the warm sand and started epic sand castles.

A bird called once, the harsh sound cutting across the gentle rhythm of the waves. Palm trees rattled their fronds, and the sweet fragrance of frangipani mixed with the salt of the sea. Mia breathed deeply, feeling her body ease into relaxation.

After a while, she rose and started toward the Yellow Bells cottage, enjoying the meandering paths winding under the coconut palms. Deep purple shadows patterned the path with palm fronds. Small lizards scuttled across the smooth concrete and birds sang overhead. A jeweled hummingbird swooped across her path with an audible whistle of speed, beelining for a large red hibiscus flower.

Yellow Bells Cottage was a charming white frame building at the very end of the line of cottages. True to its name, it was framed by two large yellow bells bushes, covered in fragrant sunshine yellow flowers, brightly dancing in the breeze. Mia climbed the stairs, breathing in the lovely smell.

The cottage was built on low stilts, raised up a little above storm tide level. Her diminutive front porch, complete with rocking chairs and rope hammock piled with yellow cushions, looked out on the vast sweep of ocean. Clever planting and generous spacing made each cottage feel completely isolated, alone in the tropical jungle. Not another soul could be seen, just sea and sky and the deep green of palm trees. Mia stretched her hands out on the white porch railing and breathed in the salt air in a huge draught, enjoying her vacation already.

The dollhouse of a cottage was charming inside as well, with white painted rafters and a slow ceiling fan stirring the air. Tall shutters framed each window, ready to shut out rain or the summer sun. Thoughtfully placed chairs dotted the room, covered by cheerful yellow flowered chintz. There was a tiny kitchen, more of an expanded wet bar, really, and a separate bedroom, with that sublime ocean view and a tall four poster bed. She pushed back the shutters, opening the entire wall of the bedroom to the gorgeous blue sea.

Mia's luggage was stacked neatly next to the closet. Methodically, she unpacked everything, storing her bags in the closet as she emptied each. She shook out hanging clothes, separating out what needed ironing— mostly the linens—and placed her other clothes into the bureau. Her extensive trip wardrobe was largely turquoises and blues with the occasional dash of rose pink, in planned coordination with the resort's color scheme. She enjoyed dressing to fit locations and occasions as much as she had back when she was a girl playing dress up in her mother's finery.

She always brought everything she might possibly want with her on trips since so much of the time, she didn't know when she would be back home in Atlanta. Mia kept bags for specific climates neatly labeled and packed in her condominium that her kids could send on to her if she needed to go straight to another hotel with a different climate. She didn't want to end up in Alaska with only her Caribbean wardrobe!

Mia and her husband, Leo Spinel, had travelled the world for the family business, setting up new hotels, updating older ones and generally checking that every last detail was perfect at the Spinel Resorts. Now that she was a widow, she continued the adventures on her own.

Mark and Alec, her stepsons and respectively, CEO and COO of Spinel Resorts, and her daughter Nicole, moving rapidly up through the company's accounting department, actively encouraged Mia to travel, not stay home and brood. Not that she was the brooding type. Mia preferred to keep busy and enjoy life to the fullest.

Of course, Mia thought with a smile, if she was busy traveling, she wasn't busy finding nice people for her children to date, and generally doing her very best to improve their lives. They did so like her to travel—and she always sent back wonderful presents.

She neatly placed the rest of her luxurious silk lingerie in soft shades of pastels into a drawer and closed it, walked out onto the porch and admired the view again. She had to admit to herself, this time her children had been right—not that she'd ever admit it to them.

Transforming the Desert Sunrise Resort into a hotel for the family to be proud of had been much more difficult than she'd anticipated, and the onsite murder hadn't helped to improve the image. It had taken longer than she expected, but by the time she left, glowing reviews of the resort were already appearing prominently, and the murder was merely intriguing history, not a deterrent to visitors.

Luckily, the Spinel Reef Resort was impeccably run, they'd assured her the balance sheets were well into the black and there wasn't a thing for her to do but vacation.

She fully intended to enjoy these next few weeks basking in this island paradise.

2

Mindful Meditations

Mia left the shutters open that night, falling asleep to the soothing sound of ocean waves under the moonlight, and waking to chirping birds welcoming the first rays of dawn. For a minute she lay in the comfortable bed, nestled below smooth white sheets, enjoying the dappled light dancing through the picture window. Finally, she stretched deeply and slowly sat up. She felt refreshed after a sound night's sleep. Now, she was ready to explore the island.

Mia quickly dressed in white linen trousers and a turquoise blouse, embroidered with brilliantly colored flowers around the neckline. With deliberation, she left her phone and her delicately jeweled watch on her bedside table, determined to not even think about work today. She was here for vacation only, Evie and Buck were taking care of the hotel. She carefully placed a pair of azure blue spinel earrings in her ears, smoothed a delicate pink lipstick over her lips and went out to start her day.

It was still early in the morning for sleeping vacationers. She couldn't hear any sounds from other guests, just the gentle breeze and soft slapping of the waves. The air felt quiet and calm, as if she was the only one awake on the island. Since she was still early for breakfast, she decided to leisurely make her way down the beach toward the main hotel. It was just a short way to the beach, down a softly trodden path fringed with grasses.

Carrying her turquoise bead adorned sandals in one hand, she rolled up her pants legs a few turns at the start of the sand, enjoying the feeling of sand sliding beneath her feet. She dug her rose pink painted toes deep into the sand, smiling at the impressions they made as the surf splashed over them. There was something about playing barefoot in the sand at the beach that took her back to childhood.

The waves gently embraced the shore, returning to the sea with a soft musical fizz as they left the sand. Mia breathed the salty air in deeply, relaxing into the soft rhythm of the ocean. The sun slowly rose, bathing the shining beach in gentle golds.

Each step on an ocean beach was a voyage in time. People had walked like this for millennia, easing their minds and bodies in the endless cycle of the sea. All she could hear was the gently splash of the waves in turquoise water. She walked meditatively, lost in the ancient call of the ocean.

The body on the beach was a shock.

A man's body lay still, just above the high tide mark. His neatly trimmed beard was encrusted in sand, but his head was horrible. Mia glanced once and turned away, feeling bile rise acidly in her throat. She gagged once, then clamped her lips down sharply, looking around for help.

The only nearby building was the dive shop, still shuttered for the night. No one was on the dock, so she walked as quickly as she could to the main hotel. Hopefully, Evie would be at work early and could call the authorities and rope off the area before someone else found the still body with its head caved in. Mia shuddered hard and moved faster.

She burst into the hotel, panting a little, and went straight to the concierge's desk. Luckily, Sandra was on duty. "Is Evie in?" Mia demanded in a rush.

Sandra looked at her curiously, as if she'd like to ask what was wrong, but confined herself to, "Any minute now. Can I help?"

As Mia was deciding what was best to do next, Buck arrived. "Hi Mia, what's going on?" He studied her a minute and frowned. "You look upset," he stated.

"I am upset," Mia's lips twisting in a tight grimace. "Buck, there's a dead man lying on the beach, down near the dive shop."

"A dead man? On our beach?" He looked at her with an odd, considering expression. "Are you sure, Mia?"

"Yes, Buck, I'm sure," she said, still feeling the shock of discovery. Her legs ached with adrenaline and her stomach churned. "Where's Evie? The local authorities need to be contacted right away," she ordered. "And we need to set up some kind of barrier. Keep guests from seeing." She shook a moment, then regained control. "It's truly horrible."

He nodded sharply, once, his mind already planning his order of operations.

"A dead body?" Sandra exclaimed with horror, standing up in surprise, then falling back into her chair. "Muddasick! Oh, my Lord in heaven!"

"Keep quiet, don't disturb the guests," Buck hissed at her. "Okay, Mia, let's go see. I really hope you're wrong, and it's just some drunk sleeping it off. They do that sometimes."

"Don't I wish," she agreed. She'd like nothing more than to be mistaken.

They left Sandra still crossing herself and talking to saints, but quietly to an empty lobby.

As they opened the doors, they ran into Evie, cheerfully smiling a greeting. "Hi, Mia, how'd you sleep?" she asked cheerily. Her expression changed, plump cheeks deflating in concern, as she saw Mia's face. "What's wrong?"

"I found a dead man on the beach," Mia said quietly.

Evie's lips made a round, silent o, her face growing pale under her rosy makeup. She dropped the cheerfully flowered bag she held and grabbed at the doorframe, holding onto it for support, then slowly straightened.

"Let's go," Buck said shortly. He moved purposefully toward the beach and dive shop, trailed by Mia and Evie.

"A man, you said? A dead man on my beach?" Evie was aghast, her plump legs moving fast in the slipping sand. "Terrible, this is terrible. We can't let the guests see."

Mia trailed reluctantly behind them, keeping her eyes glued to her feet in their turquoise sandals, deliberately trudging through the white sand. She didn't want to see the dead man again.

"There's no one here," Buck sharply called ahead. "Are we in the right place?"

Reluctantly, Mia looked up. Nothing but pristine beach in either direction. She hurried down, scouring the sand. "Yes, yes, this is it." She looked around and saw nothing but white sand, covered by the day's footprints. "I don't understand."

Buck scanned the nearby scenery, "Nothing's here, Mia. Was he in the water? Did he float away?" His eyes inspected the tide.

Evie looked like what she really wanted to do was collapse on the beach in relief. Prevented by wanting to keep her bright dress sand free, she fanned herself rapidly with her hand. "Oh, Mia, you really had me scared."

"But there was a body on the beach, not in the water," her voice squeaked, and she cleared her throat. Mia looked around, triangulating where she had stood, and moved a few feet over. "Here," she pointed to a scuffled area in the sand. "It was right here." She pointed again. "You can see my footprints, below the high tide line." Her meandering line of footprints at the surf's edge had stopped, making two deep footprints in the sand where she had stood in shock, then veered off toward the hotel, carefully skirting the area of disturbed sand. Below the high tide line was smooth and undisturbed. Above high tide was impossible to tell, the sand pockmarked with footprints, new and old.

Buck looked at her and her footprints, then went over to check the thick bushes at the edge of the beach. Nothing. He unlocked the dive shop, quickly glancing inside the tiny beach hut. "No one here. And all the equipment's still locked up tight." He relocked the door and checked behind the shack. Returning, he looked at her with deep concern. "Mia, there's no body."

She frowned. "No, there's not," she agreed. There certainly wasn't.

"Maybe someone was sleeping on the beach?" Evie suggested. "Guests, they do that sometimes." She shook her head. "We tell them, stay in your room where it's nice, no lizards in your pants legs. But sometimes, they get drunk, and we find them out in the sand." She shook her braided crown again at the odd things hotel guests did.

"He wasn't asleep," Mia stated.

"Could be someone collapsed after an early swim," Evie tried again. "We've had several people barely pull themselves out of the water, especially first day or two here. Still pretty cold water here, this early in the season. And a lot of guests aren't used to swimming much."

"No," Mia said. She baldly stated, "His head was all bloody." She shuddered once, hard, clamping down on the rising bile. "He had to have been dead. No one could live with that much blood."

"Did you check for a pulse?" Buck asked. "Head wounds do bleed a lot."

"No," Mia told him. "I didn't." She pointed at her footprints, far short of the disturbed sand. "I hurried to get help."

"The man must have been injured, not dead," he told her. "From what Mark said, you've been coming across so many dead bodies recently, it's no wonder you assumed he was dead." He examined the disturbances in the white sand in front of him, reading its story. "I don't see any blood on the ground, but that doesn't mean too much. If someone was badly injured, they'd scuff up anything just getting to their feet." He looked at the dock. "Not far away from the dive area. Maybe someone hit their head and just made it to the beach, collapsed, then went to find help."

"Wouldn't he have gone to the hotel?" Mia asked uncertainly. "There aren't footprints toward the hotel in the high tide line. Just mine." Pristine smooth sand, marred only by Buck and Mia's footprints, lay on the island side of the scuffed area.

"Might be staying in a cottage or just wanted to get to his room quickly. Could have circled back through the surf and gone up the beach. You have a head injury; you do all sorts of odd things." Buck gestured along the shoreline. "Several paths through the brush to guest rooms. Just because he didn't head straight there doesn't mean he didn't circle back this way. Groundskeepers haven't been by to sweep the beach yet, so hard to tell what's this morning or last night."

"We need to do an immediate well check on all guests," Evie decided. "It was a man you saw?"

Mia said slowly, "A caucasian man with medium length dark hair and a short clipped beard." She thought back, reluctantly pulling up the terrible picture in her head. "He was wearing long khaki shorts and a pink polo shirt, not wet but very sandy."

"A white man with a beard," Evie said, mentally taking down the description. "Well, that's something to go on. We'll do an immediate well check on any guests with beards." She thought a minute. "No one on our team with a beard, short or long."

"A short beard could also be simply scruffy from several days vacation as well," Buck reminded her. "Lots of men don't bother to shave on vacation. So you should check on all white males." He looked at Mia. "Old or young?"

Mia held up her hands and dropped them. "I don't know. Middle aged, maybe?" He'd mostly looked sickly gray. She hadn't noticed wrinkles.

"So very old or very young is unlikely, but still everyone should be checked. And don't forget blonde hair often looks dark when wet, Evie."

"Check discretely," Mia said. "I don't want word getting around about a missing body. No point in guests being disturbed by what must have been an unfortunate injury." She shook her head. "He looked so dead. I just can't understand it." She clenched her hands, feeling the tips of her well manicured nails just biting the skin. "I just don't understand. I saw him here, bloody and awful." She shook her head, dazedly. "I feel terrible for not checking for a pulse. Letting him wander off on his own."

"Don't worry, Mia. You did the right thing to go for help." Evie smiled thinly. "I'll tell the team you found someone hurt on the beach, and they had left by the time you got back with help." She shrugged her round shoulders with decision. "It's what must have happened."

"I'll tell Sandra that's what happened," Buck added. "No other explanation, really." He smoothed his silver hair. "You sure you really saw him, Mia? You've been finding a lot of bodies lately and that sort of thing gets to you after a while."

Carefully not looking at Mia, Evie pinned a braid back into her crown that had fallen loose in her rush.

"Buck, I saw a man with a horribly bloody head lying on the beach, completely still and pale as a ghost." She looked around, shrugging a little at the empty beach. "Since he's not here, I suppose you must be right. He must have made it off the beach, at least, so he couldn't have been dead." She shivered, remembering the head wound. "He certainly looked dead, though. The poor man."

Buck looked at her with obvious concern. "You've got this under control, Evie, right?"

"No problem. Well checks are standard operating procedure. Happens every so often, eh." She patted Mia's arm kindly with a plump, reassuring hand. "Not nice for you to have a fright like that, but we'll take care of it. Don't you worry about a thing."

"Let me walk you back to your cottage, Mia." Buck held out a crooked arm and she took it. "Send a good breakfast along, huh, Evie? I'm starving."

"Will do." Evie trotted with renewed vigor up the slight slope to the hotel, her solid bulk moving easily beneath her bright print dress.

"Back by the beach?" he asked.

"The beach will be fine," Mia agreed.

For the first few hundred feet, she peered into the undergrowth, looking for some sign of the man's body. No footprints beside traces of her own marred the smooth surface of the high tide line.

Buck was not unobservant. "No sign of a body, huh?"

She shrugged noncommittally. "Not a thing."

"I'll make sure the landscapers check the beach edges, and I'll check the paths on my way back. Be awful if that man staggered off in the wrong direction and fell into the bushes." He frowned at the smooth sand stretching out. "I don't see any signs of that, though."

Mia imagined an injured man, trapped in the vines and thorny undergrowth. She shivered hard, suddenly cold under the rising sun.

"Don't worry, Mia," Buck told her, wrapping an arm around her, warming her. "An injured man would have left a trail in the sand, and I didn't see any signs of one. It's just good to double check everything when someone is hurt."

"You're right, he would have left a trail you could follow." Navy Seals didn't miss trails in the sand.

"The sand was pretty scuffed up, so I think the poor guy had a badly bleeding head wound, but managed to get to his feet, then along the surf edge to his room. I expect he took the other direction—we wouldn't see traces if he made it to one of the docks. Lots of traffic to and from those," Buck reassured her. "Evie will find him and make sure he's okay."

Mia agreed, "You're right. It's the only possible explanation." She shivered again. "He just looked so dead, so pale."

Buck swung his arm around her shoulders. "Mia, you've seen a few too many dead bodies lately. You saw someone badly injured and just assumed it was another one."

"I suppose." Mia didn't understand how she could had made such a terrible mistake, but she must have. It was the only logical explanation.

Buck hugged her reassuringly with one muscular arm as he dropped her off at her cottage. "I'd stay for breakfast, but I want to check those paths out asap."

"I'm fine, Buck. Just find that poor man and make sure he's okay. I'll see you later today and hear the news," she told him.

As Evie came back into the hotel, she gave an audible sigh of relief. Sandra looked at her, concerned, "Is he really dead? Should I call an ambulance? Or can we get him to hospital faster on a boat? I didn't like to call for help until I knew what shape he was in." Her hands twisted together, long nails clinking.

"Neither," Evie shook her head. "Thank goodness, no one was on the beach."

"But Mia said—" Sandra began.

"The poor man must have been injured, but made it off the beach when Mia came in here. Probably headed straight for his room." Evie shrugged expressively, round shoulders rolling under her cheerfully printed dress. "Mia walks fast for her age, but she doesn't exactly sprint, you know."

"Pretty fast for an injured man, though," Sandra frowned.

"My guess is he wasn't as bad hurt as Mia thought. You know, she's seen a lot of problems lately. I think she saw someone with blood on his head from a cut and assumed the worst. Scalp wounds can bleed a lot and scare the living daylights out of you." Evie shook her head again. "I remember when my nephew got hit with a ball. Blood everywhere and my sister fainted dead away. He was fine after a few stitches." Evie smoothed her braids. "Mia really didn't need to start her vacation with that kind of a shock."

"But if a man is badly injured?"

"We'll do the usual well check, focusing on white males. Do you know any with beards? Mia thought he had a short beard. Or possibly just scruffy."

Sandra shrugged, sending her shining gold earrings sparkling. "I can't think of any off the top of my head." She tapped on her keyboard.

"We'll, ask around and hopefully we find the injured man quickly, see if he even needs our help. Tell the groundskeepers to do a quick sweep between the beach and the rooms. If the man collapsed on the way to his room, we need to find him quickly." Evie pursed her lips, then relaxed them. "If he was that quick, he's probably fine, eh? But good to check."

Sandra smiled, accepting the explanation, then winked broadly at Evie. "Ask Henry if he saw an injured man. He usually walks down the beach in the morning."

Evie carefully kept her face expressionless. "That's an idea, but hopefully we'll find the poor man with a quick well check. Don't want to wake sleeping guests though."

"No, let them lie. We'll see them all eventually at breakfast." Sandra pulled a paper out of the printer. "Here's a guest list of all male guests currently staying. I'll start by checking off early diners. I'll ask the resort team to report as they see people, check them off our list."

"Thanks, Sandra. Let me know as soon as you've found him and made sure he's all right." Evie escaped into her office with a feeling of relief.

What a way to start a morning, she thought, placing her nose in a vase of fragrant frangipani, breathing in the rich floral scent. Calming down, she looked out on the marina from her picture window. People were just starting to move around the beach. An early dive group, still yawning, trudged down the dock, weighted down by their heavy gear. Evie smiled a little. She'd have waited until after coffee, herself. Chef Louis started up his little motorboat, heading for the morning markets, as he did every morning.

She sat down, trying to concentrate on her paperwork. Mia visiting was always a disruptive element to the hotel. Not necessarily a bad element—Evie loved her like an aunt. Mia had taken a big chance on her, a woman with no fancy degrees to run her hotel, when Evie had only worked at Spinel Resorts a few years. Evie had made sure that Mia's gamble had paid off—she'd done her very best and put in the long hours to make the hotel a success. Both Mia and Evie had been rewarded. She considered Mia her mentor and a good friend, now, after so many years of facing challenges together.

However, Mia never came to stay without leaving changes in her wake. She'd convince Louis to alter the restaurant menus. She'd have walls repainted in different colors on the spur of the moment—and Evie would feel lucky she hadn't had those walls moved. She'd hang local art she'd found in the lobby, changing the careful interior designer's scheme. One time, Evie had come out to find Mia ordering half the tables on the terrace moved to the beach.

It wasn't that they were bad things—the tables had worked better where she put them. But it had made lunch that day half an hour late and she'd abruptly relocated several guests relaxing in the morning sun. Mia stirred things up whenever she came.

No one could pry into the personal life of employees and guests quite like Mia. Evie smiled at the memory of several couples who'd began as impromptu and unwitting victims at Mia's dinner table. She'd convinced people she was sure were meant to be together onto long boat rides, trapped them as dive buddies and, on one notable occasion, marooned a couple together on a desert island for the day. No one could be more tenaciously devious than Mia when she felt two people truly belonged together.

Evie rubbed her temples, feeling her head start throbbing. She hoped they'd find the injured man soon, before Mia started banging on guests' doors, for their own good. Actually, Evie couldn't believe Mia had returned to her cottage so meekly. Evie suddenly frowned. It really wasn't like Mia to give up so easily.

Mia tried not to think of the poor man at all during breakfast. She was certain Evie would find the injured man, and make sure he got whatever treatment he needed. If he was hurt badly enough, she would see the air ambulance helicopter arrive. She still didn't understand why the poor man had seemed so very dead, lying there on the beach, but she must have made a mistake. And it was a good thing Evie was looking for a live guest versus a dead one. A very good thing. She really didn't want any more deaths in her hotels.

So she slowly savored her excellent breakfast on the little porch, brought to her by a smiling young woman. Elizabeth had told her all about her boyfriend on the mainland, "Still working hard in school, Ms. Mia. He's going to be a doctor soon and we'll get married." She confided, "He's already helped with my auntie's bad knee. She can go up and down steps, no problem, now."

Still piping hot after the short journey, buttery crêpes held perfectly scrambled eggs. Two slices of bacon were crisply delicious. And toast with guava jam was the ideal finishing touch. After she had eaten everything on the beautifully laid tray, she felt a little more able to face the day.

Stretching, she placed her hands on the white porch railing. Her muscles had tensed after the sudden shock this morning and she twisted her neck from one side to the other. Perhaps there was an opening in the yoga on the beach class this morning. Deep stretches and meditation to the sound of waves would be a good way to reset her day to full enjoyment of her trip. She looked out at the endless ocean, her heart calm and at peace again.

The first sign of anything worrying was the uncertain look Sandra gave her as Mia approached the concierge desk. She'd chosen a hot pink headscarf today, as bright and cheery as her turquoise shirt. Large pink sparkly beads adorned her wrists, coordinating with her exquisitely manicured nails. The bright colors belied the little furrow growing between Sandra's eyebrows as she looked with concern at Mia. "Ms. Mia, you okay?"

"I'm fine, but a little stiff. Too much sitting in the plane and airports, I expect." Sandra nodded to show she was listening, but the little worry furrow grew deeper. "Can you book me into a yoga class this morning? And maybe the spa this afternoon? I'd love a good massage to work out the knots."

Sandra's face relaxed a little with the easy task. "No problem, there's a beach yoga class in an hour."

"Sign me up, then. On which beach?" Mia fervently hoped it was not the beach the dead, she corrected herself firmly, the injured man had been. She'd like a good rainstorm to come through before lying down on that sand.

"Oh, it's next to the workshop center." Sandra quickly tapped at her computer, her long pink nails hitting the keys without her fingers even touching. "You're all set." She hesitated. "I think Ms. Evie was looking for you." She looked down at her desk, then back up, shrugging to separate herself from the situation. "She's in her office now."

"Just the person I wanted to see," Mia told Sandra. She went down the hall to the manager's office, catching Sandra staring after her, giving Mia an awkward smile before she abruptly looked down at her desk, face reddening. Sandra straightened her headscarf where it had whipped around too fast, an end untucking.

"Mia!" Evie stood up and came around her desk to greet her as Mia entered. Her office reflected her personality, a huge bouquet of tropical flowers on the credenza, bold, colorful paintings of oceans and flowers and all paperwork neatly filed away. "I'm so glad to see you looking well after this morning. What a start to your vacation." She shook her head at the thought.

"It was a shock, but I'm fine now," Mia said. "That delicious breakfast you sent certainly helped."

"Aren't those crêpes delicious? It's Louis' recipe, of course. I love them with mangos and chocolate for dessert." Evie patted her rounded tummy under her bright dress. "I swear, half the guests return just for his cooking, it's that good."

"I can believe it," Mia said appreciatively. "I'm looking forward to his dinner tonight."

Evie sat down at her desk and fiddled with a pen. "Mia, I don't know how to tell you this, so I'll just say it." She hesitated, rolling the pen to and fro between her plump fingers.

"Yes?" Mia encouraged, to hurry her along.

"We did a well check, all bearded male guests. I checked on them personally. Only three sporting beards, and they were all fine. No signs of any trauma at all." She frowned a little. "I didn't like to ask too many questions, you know? So I might have missed a minor injury."

"I agree. If they think they're fine and look fine, that's all that matters." Mia frowned. "What about Buck's idea of a few days beard growth looking like a short beard?"

Evie rolled her pen, pursing her full pink lips. "Yes, I thought that was worth checking too. So I got the hospitality team to do a well check on all adult males staying this week—might as well be cautious when a head injury is involved. No one showing any visible injuries." She spread her plump hands wide, welcoming any ideas. "No one at all, Mia. I can't find a single man on the island with a visible head injury."

Mia sat, stunned, for a minute.

"Can I suggest maybe the man was much less injured than you thought?" Evie grasped her pen, turning it around with her well manicured, rosy pink nails.

"I suppose that must be what happened," Mia said, not believing it for a minute, but too certain of Evie's ability to find an injured guest staying in her hotel to question it. "Could it be someone else, maybe someone trespassing on the island?"

"Anything is possible," Evie shrugged noncommittally, clearly not thinking much of the idea. "But a boat on the beach or strange person wandering around would be noticed fairly quickly, I think. It's a small island and everyone knows everyone. My team notices if guests aren't where they're supposed to be. And groundskeeping checks the paths constantly." Her pen tapped with a sharp click. "Did you notice any boats pulled up on the beach when you were walking?"

Mia thought back. "No, I didn't see any. I don't think I would have missed a boat pulled up onto the beach."

Evie turned the pen around, deliberately making a circle. "I even checked with Henry, the only other island resident, myself. He has a long beard, not short," she smiled a little, "but he was fine." She said hesitatingly, "It's possible someone played a trick on you. There are several teenagers staying here. Maybe someone thought it would be funny to play dead on the beach. Makeup and such." Her lips pursed distastefully.

Mia thought a minute. "That is possible, I suppose. It definitely was not a teenager lying there."

"Maybe one of the bachelor party groups thought it would be a clever trick after they'd had a few too many. Sometimes they get pretty rowdy. Or a drunk fell asleep on the beach and didn't want to advertise it." The pen tapped. "If the cut was under the hairline, it might not be noticeable after he cleaned up the blood. Scalp wounds bleed a lot, even when they're not serious."

"Maybe." Mia knew enough makeup tricks to doubt the man's pallor had been painted on.

"The important thing is we don't have any critically injured people on the island," Evie nodded her head. "We made sure of that."

"Yes, you've been very thorough," Mia told her. "Well, I'm not sure what was going on with the man, but he doesn't seem to be at our hotel."

"No, praise the Lord," Evie agreed fervently. "And Mia," she looked down at her pen, rolling it between her fingers, then she smiled up at Mia with her warm brown eyes, "don't worry about all of this. You've had too much stress lately. Just take a vacation and relax."

"I plan to." Mia looked up at the clock on the wall. "I'm going to go take a yoga class right now. Get all the knots out of my neck." She stretched it a little gingerly. For some reason, it had really stiffened up.

"Good, good," Evie told her. "Then have a nice lunch and just relax. Are you still up for dinner with me tonight?"

"Of course," Mia told her. " I'm looking forward to tasting Louis' cuisine again." She left Evie's office with her smile plastered to her tight face, nodding pleasantly to Sandra on her way out.

The walk from the main hotel to the workshop center was peaceful under the palm trees. Just far enough to separate the main beach flock from classes practicing yoga or learning to windsurf, neither things that were safe to do on crowded beaches.

Not that the beach here was ever too crowded, Mia thought. Even when the hotel was full, as it was now, there were only about a hundred and fifty guests and a third the number of the resort team. Not many people for an island this size. Not too many people for Evie to check on every man on the island. If she said there wasn't an injured man among her guests and resort team, there wasn't. Except Mia had definitely seen that man lying on the beach.

She decided she had done all she could about the incident. She would go to yoga, stretch and relax, and completely put this puzzle out of her head. For now.

She arrived at the charming white building shadowed by tall coconut palms. Like the other buildings, a porch with rocking chairs surrounded it, perfect for early arrivals to meditate or husbands to snooze while waiting for their wives. The workshop center was a deceptively large building, able to host conferences that included every guest on the island. Mia wondered what other classes Evie had going at the moment. She generally sampled every one when she stayed at a hotel. Currently, the building looked like it was divided into two sections, with a desk in the middle manned by a smiling young woman.

"Hi, Sharon," Mia said, reading the young woman's name tag. "We haven't met yet. I'm Mia, here to take the yoga class."

The woman's brilliant smile practically lit up the room. "Hi, Ms. Mia, nice to meet you. The changing room is that away." Sharon nodded to clearly marked doors. She pointed at a shelf with colorful towels. "You collect one of the beach towels right there. When you're done, just drop it in that basket at the door."

Mia nodded.

"They'll be starting in about ten minutes," Sharon told her. "Just head out when you're ready!"

"Thanks." After changing to her yoga clothes, Mia stepped out onto the wide deck, dotted with turquoise umbrellas and comfortable white pillowed chairs. The sky was a pastel blue, but the water shone pale green as a fluorite gemstone, sparkling under the morning sun. She slowly walked down the sandy stairs, smiling at the sea.

About ten women were gathered, awkwardly holding their towel rolls, waiting for the class to start. One woman, who certainly had the figure for it, wore a tiny hot pink bikini, but most wore expensive yoga clothes carefully designed to hide any perceived figure flaws they preferred concealing. They eyed each other warily, clearly wondering who would be the best at complex stretches in this new group. Greeting everyone with a smile, she said, "Hi, I'm Mia."

Most smiled back uncertainly, but one woman greeted her. "I'm Donna." Her softly rounded figure was in good shape for her age, but she clutched the towel in front of her stomach protectively. "Have you taken this class before?"

"Not since I was here last winter," Mia said. "Yoga on the beach is unbelievably relaxing. I think one time I just fell asleep afterwards." She laughed.

"That sounds like the perfect yoga session," a tall woman with short, no nonsense brown hair said. "I'm Carol, by the way."

"If I fell asleep on the beach, I'd burn to a crisp." Donna pointed at the pink beginnings of sunburn on her arms. "I'm coated in the highest SPF sunblock I could find today. I don't want to get stuck inside when we're only here for two weeks."

"Absolutely not," Mia agreed. "I usually wear a hat at the beach, but that doesn't exactly work with yoga. It'll fall off during downward dog and blow away." They both laughed and others joined in.

"This is such a treat for me. Usually, I'm always working." Carol barked a laugh. "I don't ever take the time for things like yoga at home. It's hard to plan for classes when you're expected to travel at a moment's notice." Carol pushed her short bangs back from her face, smiling in the ocean breeze. "Yoga on the beach sounded like the perfect relaxation to me."

"Me too. I'm looking forward to a complete renewal this trip," enthused a young woman, with recently cut hair, intensely styled and highlighted, and makeup so heavy it was hard to see her actual skin tone. Her brand new yoga clothes were designed to catch a man's, any man's, eye with plentiful cutouts in unexpected, or perhaps expected, areas that did nothing to enhance her figure, but merely advertised it. "I got my divorce last month, and I needed a total change of scenery. I put my house on the market, and escaped to the tropics to celebrate my new single life." Her brittle laugh didn't reach her mascara ringed eyes.

"What a good idea," Mia said cheerfully. "No worries about messing up the house while it's being shown, and you can decide on your fresh start."

The woman perked up visibly at the praise. "Just me, Megan, now. On my own."

"You go, girl," one of the other women spoke up. Mia recognized the woman carrying a stack of bags from her rental boat yesterday. "I'm Amy Smith. Being on your own is awesome." Mia guessed her romantic trip with her husband was probably not working out. Amy's compact, muscular figure was encased in light gray yoga clothes, with a neon green stripe running diagonally across. Her wet blond hair was scraped up into a ponytail, showing the dark roots.

"Yeah, no dirty socks on the floor," the recent divorcée agreed. "Men are pigs." Everyone laughed.

"I've never regretted my divorce." Carol added quietly, "Except for my son. Divorce is so hard on kids." She twisted her face up comically. "Of course, now he's all grown up, he leaves his socks everywhere. I try to avoid his apartment so I don't go all mom and clean up after him."

Donna added, "It's the male genes. I finally got my husband to pick up after himself now he's retired, but now my grandchildren leave toys all over the house. I'm always stepping on Legos. Talk about painful!" She smiled ruefully. "I love my family living with us, but we ran away for a vacation when they did."

"That's the only way to survive," Mia agreed. "Look, here's the teacher."

Running her hand through a curly nimbus of hair, the yoga teacher greeted them with a flash of white teeth. "Hi, I'm Julie. Prepare for a good workout, followed by complete and total relaxation." She waved hello to Mia. "Hi, Ms. Mia. Glad to see you again." She spread out her towel at the high water mark. "Okay, class, spread your towels out so you can see and follow me. Let's get strong and calm!"

The class quickly obeyed, spreading a rainbow of beach towels in front of the gentle ocean waves. Mia stretched and folded in a fluid flow, guided by Julie's serene voice. The sound of the ocean and the smooth movements of her body enveloped Mia in tranquil meditation.

3

More Questions

Mia and Donna returned together to the hotel, leisurely walking up the beach. People were exploring the island, laughing and playing, enjoying their vacation in paradise.

"That felt so good," Donna enthused. "I know I'll feel it tomorrow, but right now I feel so relaxed."

"I agree," said Mia, adjusting her glamorous sun hat to the perfect angle to shield her face from the sun. She just had to ask. "Did you arrive at the hotel yesterday? By the ferry?"

"Yes, got here yesterday on the ferry, so it's all still pretty new. I thought everyone but the rich kid in the helicopter came on the ferry then." She looked curiously at Mia. "But I guess you weren't on the ferry either."

"No, an old friend picked me up in his boat," she demurred. Interesting, Donna had noticed who had—and hadn't—traveled on the ferry. She must be more observant than Mia had assumed."Gorgeous thing, he just finished restoring it."

"Lucky you," Donna said with envy. "I love beautiful old boats. Something about the layers of varnish on warm wood. We had the most sublime sailboat once. Used to take it sailing all around the Hudson River and berth her in New York Harbor," she sighed. "That was a long time ago, pre-kids."

"It's amazing how children change your life," Mia agreed. She dove right in with the ridiculous question. "Did you notice any men with beards on the ferry?"

Donna stared at her in surprise, then thought a minute. "One, rather stout, in plaid shorts. Two, that tall man with the bright orange shirt." She closed her eyes to aid recall, then opened them. "Oh, and that creepy guy with the dive group." She closed her eyes again, reopening after a minute. "That's all, I think. Why?"

"Oh, a friend said he might arrive by the ferry yesterday. It doesn't sound like he did, from what you say." She shrugged, laughing to dispel importance. "He's absolutely terrible at remembering to give his schedule, so I'm never sure when he'll arrive."

"But surely you'd know if he checked in yesterday?" Donna's thick, gray hair swung as she looked at Mia quizzically.

"I'll ask at the desk," Mia said mendaciously, changing the subject. "What are you planning this afternoon? Do you think you might go sailing?" She smiled encouragingly. "Bring back old times, before kids?"

Donna smiled in memory, dropping her obvious curiosity about the odd question. "It's our fortieth anniversary, so we're doing absolutely everything together. Except yoga. Todd put his foot down on yoga. Like he could even touch his feet now." She giggled like a young girl. "We're going diving later on the reef." She looked a little nervous. "I haven't been in years, but the concierge said the dive guide would help. I hope I remember what to do." Her brow furrowed a little, and her mouth twisted uncertainly. "I meant to take a refresher class when Todd retired. I've just been so busy, I haven't gotten around to it." She pushed back her heavy hair from her forehead.

"Oh, you won't have any problems, they'll have someone there to make sure you're okay. And the reef here isn't too deep, so it's an easy one to reacquaint yourself on," Mia told her. "I can't wait to go myself and see how it's changed in a year. I think it's been that long since I went diving."

"I'm so glad to finally be on vacation," Donna said with a smile. "Todd has picked up some consulting work—he's in finance—just to keep busy since he retired. Between shuttling the kids and his meetings, I feel like I see him less than when he was working." Her lips pursed. "At least when he had a regular job, we scheduled date nights. Now—something usually comes up."

"Men do like to keep busy."

"So when he said let's drop everything and run away to the Bahamas together, I just packed my bags." Her wide lips grinned, rounding her pink flushed cheeks into apples. "And here we are!"

"That's wonderful," Mia agreed with appreciation. "A really romantic gesture."

"I know, so unlike him—he's usually a planner—but I love it," Donna enthused. "I hope it's the start of something new. Oh, here's Todd!" Her smile widened.

Todd, a tall, erect man with silver gray hair, and still evident muscles, muffled by a little padding, greeted Donna with a warm hug. "How was yoga, dear?"

"Perfect. Oh, Todd, this is Mia. We met at yoga."

"Nice to meet you," Todd greeted her, his body clearly telegraphing his refusal to ask her to join them at lunch. "We have reservations over there, dear. Right next to the beach," he added with pride.

Smiling a little, Mia returned the greeting and waved goodbye, to his polite, but obvious relief at finally getting his wife alone with no strangers or grandchildren underfoot. He ushered her to their table, solicitously guiding her way.

Smiling, Mia walked up the stairs to the outside tables overlooking the dive dock. "Hi, Elizabeth, I'd like a table for lunch, please."

"I have the perfect one for you, Ms. Mia. Is anyone joining you?"

"Not today."

The table was lovely, on the far side of the deck, situated with a panoramic view of the dive dock stretching across the ocean and the other diners. "Thank you, Elizabeth."

On the waitress's advice, she ordered classic Bahamian fare of conch chowder and topped it off with conch fritters. It had been a while since she'd tasted conch, at its absolute best, served fresh from the ocean. Looking out over the dive dock, she saw Buck leading a small group of exhausted divers back. Their faces were marked red by masks and respirators, but glowed from their experience.

Elizabeth brought her the fritters first, golden brown and piping hot. She bit into one, the crisp outside breaking to reveal the delicious mix of conch, onions, peppers and celery inside. She dunked the next into the dipping sauce, spicy and spiked with bright lime juice. "Elizabeth, these are scrumptious." Mia ate another. "Please tell chef they're even better than last year."

She beamed back at Mia, "Oh, I know they are." She leaned in close, whispering conspiratorially. "My best guess is some kind of marinade, but they are so, so good. I can't stop eating them."

Mia ate another. "I agree completely."

Elizabeth bustled off, fielding her large tray through the tables with practiced ease.

Mia savored each delicious bite, letting her eyes wander around the outdoor restaurant. Most of the women from the yoga class were having lunch here. Donna, of course, was eating with her husband, both leaned in close and talking with tender smiles meant just for each other.

Amy had changed into unflattering baggy khaki shorts and a navy polo shirt, but still hadn't brushed out her straggly ponytail. Mia sincerely hoped she was saving styling for a salon appointment later in the day.

Amy, unfortunately, was not exchanging affections with her spouse. They were both sitting upright, barely bothering to glance at each other. Her husband, briskly tapping at his phone with a frown on his face, wore a tight shirt barely fitting around his gym-sculpted biceps. His smoothly tanned cheeks showed just a hint of dark stubble, with edges meticulously defined. His dark hair swept back from his forehead in a fastidious wave that must take a lot more time to maintain than Amy's quick ponytail. His darkly lashed eyes didn't even glance in Amy's direction. If they hadn't just had an argument, Mia would be very surprised.

Mia didn't think the recent divorcée, Megan, would remain single permanently, despite her fervent praise of the single life. With a predatory eye, she evaluated every man who walked by, clearly summing up the male's plusses and minuses in her head. A female companion didn't seem to change the respective totals much. She was definitely on the prowl.

The young woman in the pink bikini splashed merrily in the ocean. She really had worn the perfect outfit for yoga on the beach, Mia thought. Simply jump in the ocean, rinse off the sand and walk back along the beach. She might wear her own bathing suit (a comparatively modest turquoise one piece) instead of yoga clothes next time.

Sighing in contentment, Mia bit into another conch fritter. It made a satisfying crunch. She really felt worlds better after taking that class.

Now, she could solve the puzzle of the disappearing man without any stress. The shock of finding the body and then losing the body had left her rather upset before. Sometimes, the best thing to do was to take a step back before starting to work a problem.

"Hi, Mia," Buck pulled out a chair and sat down heavily, uninvited. "Can I join you?" he asked belatedly, catching her look.

"You may," Mia said guardedly. Buck was going to be a problem, she just knew it. "How was your dive?"

"Pretty good," he looked up at Elizabeth hovering for his order. "The usual, please." He returned his gaze to Mia. "Some grunts and butterfly fish. Sea turtle. A good day."

"Maybe you can take me diving tomorrow?"

"Absolutely. Private dive for you too." Buck shoved at the arms on his chair, pushing himself back in his chair. "Look, Mia, I talked to Evie."

"Yes?" she gazed at him with limpid blue eyes, not volunteering a thing.

"You know there's no one on the island that's hurt," he said awkwardly. He twisted his icy glass around on the table, enlarging the condensation ring.

"No guests or hospitality members on the island are visibly injured," she corrected him. "I am sure Evie did a very thorough well check. She's extremely efficient." She added, "I'm so glad I chose her for manager here. Really, she thinks of everything."

Buck refused the misdirection. "Well, then," he stopped, clearly unsure what to say. He swiped his hand over his short hair.

"Yes?"

"You can't have seen an injured man on the beach," he said with exasperation, thumping his arm rests in emphasis. "Look, Mia, the thing's impossible."

"Absolutely," she agreed demurely, enjoying his reddening face. It clashed terribly with his silver hair.

"So you couldn't have seen it." He was having trouble keeping his voice low. Mia felt glad Elizabeth's table choice was a little isolated. She disliked public arguments.

She made no reply since there wasn't really one she could make. She wasn't going to say she hadn't seen the body, when she had.

"Look, Mia, I know you've found a lot of dead bodies lately," he began.

"Oh, I haven't actually found many of them, not personally," she corrected. "They've been found at hotels I stayed at. Found by other people. Finding them would be completely different," she informed him calmly, while inwardly shuddering at the memory of that man's bloody head, washed by sand. Once was enough.

He ignored her protestations. "And I saw a lot of this in the teams, you know. Men would think they were still at war when they were safe at home. It's hard to get over some stuff." He eyed her uncertainly. "It happens, you know."

"Buck, don't be absurd." She looked directly at him with suddenly glacier hard blue eyes. "Believe me or don't. I refuse to discuss this matter any further."

"I should tell Mark," he wavered, clearly dreading that particular conversation.

"Do whatever you want," Mia told him acerbically. "I, personally, don't think you should worry him unless there's something to worry about." She added pertly, "He's had to deal with several murders at his hotels lately, you know."

Buck just looked at her.

"I am going to enjoy this delicious conch chowder. I suggest you enjoy your lunch as well," she said, as Elizabeth placed her steaming bowl in front of her with a flourish.

Beach Day

After lunch, Mia adjourned to the beach, leaving Buck sourly eating his fish. She found a good vantage point for people watching under a shady umbrella. In just a minute, George was at her side with a frosty, tart switcha. "Is there anything else you'd like, Ms. Mia?"

"No, thank you, George. I just had a wonderful lunch. I'm going to enjoy the beach for a few minutes." She smiled up at him. "When you have a minute, please do join me."

George nodded. "Let me take care of my guests, then I'll be right back." His tall, straight backed figure moved through the crowd with the dignity of a general marshaling his forces.

Contentedly sipping her switcha, Mia looked around. Behind her big sunglasses, the bright sun cooled, kissing the beach with warm rays and setting the diamonds sparkling on the water. Many of the same people she'd seen at lunch and arriving yesterday were relaxing on the beach. Everything seemed much the same as usual. The diving group shepherded by Buck were playing beach volleyball, as badly as yesterday, and having just as much fun in their silly game. She counted one bearded guest in that group, but he was definitely not the man she'd seen on the beach. He was, ahem, rather large for that, with a distinctly flabby gut.

Bright turquoise umbrellas dotted the white sand, laid out in small groups of two or four lounge chairs, with a few single chairs for more solitary guests spaced at the outskirts of the main beach area. The long dive dock stretched far out into the little bay. She couldn't see the marina docks in the distance except for bobbing masts against the blue sky.

She watched with interest as Dr. Barbeau and his graduate student emerged from the water, climbed the dock ladder, hauling up their dive flag and several heavy mesh sample bags behind them. After sloughing off their dive gear, they tramped down the long dock, clearly exhausted after their research work. They must have been out all morning. The student dragged a small cart behind them, filled with their equipment and sample bags.

What could they possibly need that many samples for? Were they testing the water quality? They shouldn't be sampling fish or corals from the nascent reef. They were just supposed to track arrivals at the emerging reef, not harass the wildlife. Mia thought she needed to schedule that talk with Dr. Barbeau.

George, carrying a tall glass of switcha of his own, sat down on the neighboring chair with a sigh of relief, leaning back on the lounge cushion. "Good to get my feet up after the lunch hour. You would think people would sit down, have a proper lunch at a table, but so many stay on the beach and have their lunch brought to them. Sand gets in all the food and then they complain about it."

"Guests don't like to miss a minute of their beach time," Mia said. "You get to enjoy it all year."

He took a long drink, supple fingers marking the condensation on his glass. "We are the lucky ones, that's for sure." He brushed sand off his khaki shorts. "Still, go on a beach picnic and accept the sand or dine at a table, like a civilized person."

Mia laughed. "I quite agree. But what the guest wants—"

"The guest gets," George chuckled as he completed her statement.

"So what are you doing out on the beach today? You don't usually have to deal with the picnickers." George was the headwaiter at the main hotel restaurant, Fritters, though he was often on hand to help with new arrivals or fill in for an absent waiter. Everything about the dining experience on the island was George's domain.

He nodded over at Skip Wilson's party, commanding their section of beach. "Evie asked me to keep them happy. We all have to keep the social publicity people happy. Influencers," he added with disgust. "That boys' club there has the potential to turn a little awkward. I didn't want Elizabeth to have to deal with rowdy young men."

Mia nodded understandingly. George watched over his waiters like a mother hen with her chicks.

Turning his glass around in his hands, he asked, "So, I heard about some confusion this morning. Everyone's curious about what happened." He was too polite to ask if she had really found an injured man or a dead one on the beach, leaving the explanation open to her.

Mia laughed. "I expect Sandra said I'd been seeing things."

He raised a heavy eyebrow, saying nothing.

"I'd like to know what's going on as well, George. I can't figure it out." Mia sipped her drink and crossed her legs, leaning confidentially toward him. "Anything unusual you've noticed about the guests staying here now? I doubt much happens on this island you don't know about. Waiters see and hear everything."

"That they do, Ms. Mia, that they do." He leaned back in his chair, crossing his legs in front of him, surveying the beach. "I heard you were looking for men with beards."

"A man, with a short beard or maybe a few days growth."

"I get it. Hard to tell which." George inspected the guests again. He nodded at Amy and her husband, lying side by side on sun chairs. "That one was smooth as a baby yesterday evening and he'll qualify for a beard in a week or two." The angular lines of the husband's evenly tanned skin were softened by a day's scruffy growth. He had an athletic figure, long and lean, with hard muscles, like a cat. The couple both read their books intently, not talking or glancing at each other, Amy glued to her iPad and her husband alternated turning the pages of a paperback spy thriller or drinking a tall frosty drink. "Those two aren't getting along. Nothing but silence or arguments. He talks a lot about going diving, brought a big bag of gear with him, but hasn't gone yet."

"Maybe he's planning to dive later today," Mia suggested.

"Maybe," George drew the sound out. "Maybe, but he hasn't signed up yet. Sandy," his smile grew wide, "that's my girlfriend—she cleans that section. She says his equipment is old old, like from some junk shop. Rent better stuff at the dive shop any day."

"Odd," Mia mused, filing away the name Sandy and girlfriend. She would make sure she met George's girlfriend this trip.

"But no beard and no head wound. So not your man," George looked hard at her for a reaction.

"I'm not sure what I'm looking for right now," Mia told him, with truth. "I think I just want to hear about anything odd on the island, even things just a little unusual."

"Guests do weird things all the time."

"Don't I know it," Mia said with feeling.

George's eyes crinkled into little folds, then he contemplated the beach goers again. "That Dr. Barbeau, he works all the time. Even has most of his dinners in his cottage. We could feed him sawdust—he wouldn't know the difference." He shook his head. "No fun at all, that one. When I bring his dinner, try to be neighborly since he's here so long, he covers up his papers, closes his computer, like I want to read a bunch of science nonsense about the reef. I live here—I know my island better than he does, eh." He was clearly annoyed with Dr. Barbeau.

"Very rude," Mia agreed. "I suppose he is on a tight schedule. His residency program here ends soon. He's back at his university next semester."

"No fun at all," George repeated disparagingly. "Plenty of scientists come here, work hard, then relax some, have a nice dinner with everyone together in the evening. Laugh, make new friends. That's what it's all about. Josh, that's the student who follows him around, he treats the same way. Closes everything when he comes in the room. How's the kid supposed to learn if his teacher hides everything from him?" He shook his head and took a gulp of his drink. "That's odd, if you like."

"What about Skip Wilson?" Mia asked with simple curiosity.

"Man, if I had a helicopter at that age, I'd have brought some friends for a party. What's he do? He sits in his room most of the day staring at a computer screen. Didn't even bring a girlfriend along. And what'd he order last night for dinner? Pizza. World class restaurant, fresh fish straight from the sea, and he wants pizza." George sighed in intense pain. "He could have stayed at home for all he's seen of the ocean." He looked at Mia and nodded at the group. "Look at them, beautiful beach, fine girls in bikinis, and they're staring at screens. What a waste." He shook his head sadly, then looked at Mia. "No beards on the men or the women," he gave a chuckle, "with him, either."

"Are there any unauthorized visits to the island?" With George's carefully blank look, she reworded the question. "Anyone who quietly visits a friend on the island and maybe doesn't want to dock at the marina with all the guests?" He visibly hesitated. She added, "I mean, one of the hospitality team inviting someone to their home during their off hours seems perfectly natural to me. Or someone having a guest visit for a few days. It's their home, after all. They live here. Of course they'd have friends to stay sometimes. But I would think a guest's boat would be docked at the marina?" Most of the resort team lived in apartments and cottages at the far end of the island. It was one of the major perks of the job.

"Yes, yes, I see," George tried to frame his wording in the right light for the hotel owner. "No one can land on the far side of the island. Too strong currents for most small boats, you might be swept into the Atlantic even."

"That certainly limits the possible boat landings to the beach."

"Mostly when people have guests, they just use the marina like the guests. Evie doesn't mind—it's the only marina and a few of us have boats. Maybe someone might beach on the sand if the marina was full up with guests or—" George broke off as a thought came to him.

"Yes?" Mia urged.

"Or if he'd been told to stay off the island," George said reluctantly, eyes averted.

"I see." Mia asked, "Is there someone who's been told to stay off the island?"

George hesitated, then shrugged. "I guess it doesn't matter so much. Ruth, you remember Ruth, works in the spa?"

"I remember Ruth. Very nice woman. Excellent masseuse."

"She had a terrible boyfriend. Now ex-boyfriend, naturally. He showed up at the hotel, drunk, calling her all sorts of names. Disgusting bit of work." He shrugged. "We got him away from the guests, sobered him up enough to pilot his boat back. Ruth told him to stay away from her, and Evie said stay away from the island, because she would call the police next time. We sent him off in his boat, an old, open fishing boat."

"And did he have a beard?"

George said unhappily, "Robert's a real conchy Joe. White guy with a nasty long beard, last I looked. Could be shorter or gone now, of course. That whole mess was a few months ago."

"I see," Mia thought a minute. "So he comes back to the island?"

George pinched the bridge of his nose for a minute. "We've seen him a few times. Last time maybe a month ago. Chased him off quick, too." He looked worried. "Look, Ruth's not going to get in trouble for this, is she? It isn't her fault; she's a good woman. She dumped him when he made the scene. She'd only dated him a few times, didn't know what he was like until he showed up drunk."

"Of course not," Mia said, with surprise. "I don't see what it has to do with her."

George looked relieved.

"Except I do want Evie to call the local police and check on him. And they'll need a last known address, I expect."

George gulped his drink, clearly wishing it was spiked with rum.

"Why don't you suggest it to Evie, George? It might look better not coming from me." Less embarrassing for Mia and less trouble for George discussing the hotel gossip with Mia after Evie had officially shelved the event.

George nodded reluctantly.

"Thank you," Mia told him. "I appreciate this very much."

"Right thing to do, I guess." George looked a little less nervous. "Best to check, even if he's a—" he visibly swallowed what he was going call the man. "Stop you worrying, eh?"

"Thanks, George."

He nodded and shoved himself to his feet. "Best get it over with." Moving with smooth deliberation, he headed toward the main hotel, and Mia sat back in her chair. Here was a possible answer to the disappearing man. An alcoholic lying on a beach in a drunken stupor, waking up, then taking his boat back out to sea made sense.

They'd find the man with a phone call, and this little incident could be closed forever. Mia lay back in her chair and closed her eyes, trying to put the whole thing out of her mind.

The look on Buck's face when he tried to convince her she'd been seeing things still bothered her. It was so frustrating. She'd seen what she thought was a dead man on the beach, reported it, and the man was missing when they came back. Possibly a complicated problem to fix, but a simple incident to have witnessed.

Now Evie and Buck both thought she'd been seeing things. Mia usually never allowed herself to get upset about other people's opinions. People were entitled to their own opinions, and what they thought about her could scarcely affect her thoughts or actions.

However, Buck was one of the few people, besides her children, whose opinion did matter to her. He was unlike her husband, Leo, in so many ways, but similar in their sound core of common sense. Buck actually believing she was imagining things surprised and disturbed her. Buck really thought she'd imagined the whole thing. She had to seriously consider his suggestion that she had made a mistake, since she valued his opinion.

She had ignored Buck thinking she had gone off the deep end when there were other likely explanations, but she wasn't fine with Buck thinking she was crazy, not one little bit. Mia tried to collect her thoughts of the morning. Could she have made a mistake? Keeping her eyes closed behind her dark sunglasses, bright sun warming her bones, she pictured the man as she had seen him, lying in the sand, unmoving.

A man had lain in the sand, that was certain. Whatever Buck thought about her mental state, the disturbed area in the sand, and the evidence of her surprised sudden halt were clear. She had seen something that startled her and was actually there, as a Navy Seal could easily read. The sand told that story clearly.

Had the man been dead or merely injured? Or a drunk, like George had suggested?

She looked at her mental image. The gray white of his skin, the concave bloody dent in his skull, dark, viscous blood rimming the wound, the absolute stillness of the chest, she remembered vividly. His legs sprawled on the sand, twisted and fish belly white, dark hairs sticking out in wiry clumps, brushed with sand. His hands and arms were tucked under his torso, useless for locomotion. Surely, a man dragging himself up the beach could not end up in such contortions. He'd been dropped there, a heavy parcel waiting for its next destination.

Mia had seen a body, not a living man. She nodded to herself, keeping her eyes closed in her deliberations.

So, a dead body had disappeared, not an injured man.

First, where had he come from?

Mia was inclined to think he came from the island, not the sea. So many dense clumps of jungle like growth enveloping the paths, welcoming wildlife in their depths. It was almost impossible to see even a few feet inside. The body could easily have been concealed beneath the thick vines and bushes. Thinking back, she realized he could even have been concealed in the dive shack for the few hours between the last dive of the day and first thing in the morning, when she had seen him. The clean sweep of high tide hadn't washed the sand clean long before she found him.

He even could have been dropped on the beach by a boat. A heavy boat would have left a dent in the sand, but a skiff wouldn't have left a trace longer than a few waves ebb and flow. Or he could have been dumped on the sand, waiting for a boat. Of course, she hadn't seen a boat leaving the beach.

How long had the man been dead?

Not too long, she thought. While the full summer heat hadn't hit yet, this was a Caribbean island. Dead things—she inwardly cringed—deteriorated rapidly. She shuddered, briefly opening her eyes to the glaring sun above and closing them again. Nature claimed the dead quickly, on the island. So he'd been dead a day at the very most.

Evie and George both said he wasn't an employee. She believed them. Therefore, he was a guest or a trespasser.

Despite the red herring of Robert, the belligerent drunk, Mia inclined toward a guest. The pale pink polo shirt, the khaki shorts seemed like a guest wardrobe, not a drunk's. What she could see of the beard seemed neatly trimmed, despite the suggestion of a few days' growth. From what she had noticed, beards were uncommon on the locals—probably too hot—unless they were of the beachcomber unkempt variety.

She thought back to the confusion of departing and arriving guests yesterday. While Evie certainly knew where every guest on the island was now, would she notice if a guest had not left on the ferry, but been quietly murdered, perhaps during a last walk along the beach, conveniently near large bushes a body could be tucked under?

She thought not. Evie was busy with arrivals and departures, Mia's arrival and the VIP group on the helicopter. She certainly didn't have time to check off departing guests. She'd only notice if they didn't vacate their room in time for cleaning.

So the bearded man could have been a guest who had checked out of the hotel, but never left the island. Interesting. She needed to check for departing bearded men.

She also thought the flurry of arrivals and departures would be the best time for a murder. The staff were concentrated in several areas, the marina, hotel lobby and ferrying bags to rooms. Most people wanted to check if their bags had arrived safely and perhaps change clothes before exploring the island. It was a very busy time, but only in a few locations. Undergrowth by the beach wasn't one of them.

She opened her eyes, letting the sun warm her and the sounds of laughter and waves wash over her.

Children splashed as they built a sand castle barely out of the waves's reach. One girl, slathered in white sunscreen, meticulously carved out crenellations in the turrets. She squealed, "Be careful!" as a boy piled sand around the castle, scooping out a moat. A small boy frowned with determination as he shoveled away enough sand for a causeway to fill the moat. They all cheered as water trickled through the sand, barely coating the water side of the moat.

Extra chairs and umbrellas had been dragged over to form a large shady grouping for Skip Wilson's party, placed at a little distance from the beachgoers, just enough to deter interlopers, but not inconveniently far for waiters. Frosty concoctions topped with fruits and little colorful umbrellas sat ready to their hands, and plates of exotic nibbles lay waiting. The men wore loud Hawaiian shirts and swimsuits over their unprepossessing physiques, overtly symbolizing they were on vacation. Except they clearly weren't.

The only thing not fitting with the relaxed beach image were the laptops they squinted at. None of the group reached for a snack or looked at the ocean, remaining riveted to their screens.As she watched, Skip hissed something at Carol, from the yoga group, then thumped his chair arm, cursing loudly, making the kids building the sand castle look up in surprise and their parents glare at Skip's group.

Carol shrugged it off, closing her computer, rubbing her eyes and looking out to sea. Stretching, the older woman doffed her long red and white coverup to reveal an athletic figure encased in a swim training style bathing suit. She plunged into the ocean and popped up yards away, short dark hair sleek as a seal's. Smooth strokes moved her rapidly parallel to the beach, going far down the shore before she turned around.

If Carol worked for Skip Wilson, no wonder she had to travel so much for her job. Mia idly wondered what her job was—she seemed efficient, so perhaps a business manager? CFO? Personal assistant? She could be anything.

The security guard lounged on the edge of the group, overtly guarding the approach to Skip while actually concentrating on his video game. His muscles were bloated, inflated as if with a bicycle pump, more for show than actual use. His puffy paunch and his fish belly pasty face told his true fitness level. While his eyes were on his laptop, what chance did he have of seeing any potential threat to his boss? Maybe he was slacking off a bit, with the controlled access to the island. It wasn't like there was a high crime rate here. There wasn't any crime on the island, as far as Mia knew.

Of course, until today, Mia wouldn't have believed there could be a disappearing body on the beach.

Skip Wilson's little clique was completed by one more man, clearly more than slightly drunk, sleeping it off under the midday sun. One leg was encased by a well worn walking cast, propped on a towel. The other hung off his lounge chair. One of his friends should move an umbrella to shade him, but no one seemed to care.

The little group was completely separate from the rest of the beachgoers. No one but George approached them. Laptops shielded them from even the pretty bikini clad girls' interest or inclusion in the whoops of the volleyball game. They were marooned on their own island in the white sand.

Oh well, none of them had beards, so they weren't Mia's concern. She looked down the beach for more interesting options.

Now, this man walking up the beach had an impressive beard. It flowed beneath his battered, misshapen straw hat, fuzzy light brown streaked with gray, reaching halfway down his tanned bare chest. He wore tattered cargo shorts and nothing else, fully acclimated to the hot afternoon sun. A small pig trotted cheerfully at his side, its short legs keeping up easily with his long strides. Carefully guiding the pig around the children's sand castle, he strode up the hotel steps, the pig following him like a well trained dog. The children pointed at the pig with squeals of joy.

Mia quickly motioned George over with a look of displeasure. "George, why is there a pig going into," she emphasized, "inside my hotel?"

George laughed, showing bright white teeth against his dark skin. "Oh, that's Henry and Pig, Ms. Mia."

"Henry?"

"Henry, yes," he prompted. "He lives on the other end of the island. In that shack on the beach."

"Oh, I remember now," Mia said. "As part of the sales agreement when we bought some of his half of the island, he still lives here and uses the hotel facilities."

"That's Henry," George agreed with a warm smile. "We see him almost every day." He added darkly, "He mostly uses the bar. Has a boat in the marina," he pointed to a battered boat with peeling turquoise paint that looked very out of place among its well kept companions.

"I see." Mia thought she could explore that point later. "But a pig? A pig?" her voice grew shrill.

"Oh, she's a nice little pig. Very good girl. No," George motioned down vaguely, "unpleasantness."

"Even if she's perfectly house trained, which I cannot believe of a pig, why is she in the hotel?"

"If she's not with him, she pines for Henry." George smiled a little. "She would sit outside looking so pitiful, whining and whimpering, waiting for him. The guests, they would worry, constantly ask for a manager to help the poor little pig." He explained further, "Henry rescued her when she was so tiny." He cupped his hands to illustrate. "Just washed up on shore, pitiful little thing. So he fed her from a bottle. Naturally, he had to take her everywhere with him to feed her. Now, she won't stop going everywhere with him."

Mia didn't know what to say.

"The guests love it, Ms. Mia," George added mendaciously. "They love seeing her play like she was a little dog. She plays in the surf. Splashes and swims. Kids love it."

"I see," Mia said, unconvinced. "Well, it's local color, I suppose."

"That's the ticket," George agreed. "Something different for the guests." Closing the subject, he added, "Another switcha?"

"No, thank you, George." Mia rose and stretched. "I'm going to go enjoy the spa before dinner. Get a nice massage."

"Rest up for dinner," he urged. "Chef Louis is amazing, on his top game. A-maz-ing," he drew the word out. "I'm working there tonight, as usual."

"What would you recommend?"

"You're here for a bit, so you have time to try everything." George's white teeth flashed. "I'll think of a special treat for tonight."

"That sounds perfect."

After Mia left, Buck scooped up the last few bites of his broiled fish. It was a dish he never tired of, since it always changed with the catch of the day. Today was fresh caught grouper with a drizzle of lime.

Frowning, he looked down at Mia's absurd pink hat bobbing under the umbrella. He couldn't make up his mind whether he needed to talk to Mark about Mia or not. And what exactly would he say to Mark? He was pretty sure Mia had only seen something in her imagination, but the sand was undeniably scuffed up, and her footprints were just as if she'd stopped when she saw a body, like she said. What could he tell Mark anyway? That Mia had lost her mind? Mark was worried enough about her already.

Even if it had been Mia's imagination, what would change? She'd been stressed, and sometimes people did things under stress they'd never dream of doing a few months later. The best thing was to calm her down, reassure her that everything necessary had been done and she shouldn't worry anymore about it.

She'd seemed so certain, though. Very specific with her description of the man. Buck's eyes darted around the beach, seeing nothing out of the way. Couples sunning themselves, children playing. His eyes stopped at Skip Wilson's group. If there was a group to cause trouble, that one was it. They sat glued to their screens, ignoring the view around them. Still, they hadn't caused trouble yet. Of course, they'd just arrived yesterday.

With a sigh, Buck rose, nodding goodbye to Elizabeth. He wandered inside the hotel and sat down by Henry at the bar. "What's up?"

"Nothing much," Henry took a gulp of his rum punch.

"You go down the beach this morning?"

"Like always," Henry punctuated with another gulp.

"See anyone lying on the beach?"

Henry's eyes narrowed and his mouth drooped under his bushy beard. "Nope. What's going on? Someone sneaking on the island again?"

"Huh," Buck frowned. Just Mia's imagination, then. "Nothing, I guess. Just checking."

"Evie asked me the same thing," Henry said. "Brought me breakfast too." He patted his tanned, concave belly. "Pancakes and eggs." He looked down at his pet pig, snoring at his feet. "I sure miss bacon, but it doesn't seem right."

"Evie's bringing you meals a lot," Buck said, with a smile.

"She's a thoughtful woman, looking out for the local washed up old drunk." He swirled his glass, twisting his mouth disparagingly.

"Huh," Buck grunted. "Evie's a lot of things, but kindly looking after washed up drunks isn't one of them. You need to get your act together," he added bluntly.

Henry sipped at his rum punch, looking down as if the bottom held his reply.

A dark haired man sat down on the other side of Henry. "Hit me with something cold, quick." He nodded at Henry's cold glass. "That looks good."

The bartender obliged, "Your rum punch, sir."

"Thanks," the man said. Looking at Henry and Buck, "Man, it's hot out there." He fanned his chest, flapping his shirt.

Buck told him, "It'll cool off late afternoon. Be a nice evening."

The man shook his head. "The wife insists on sitting out there in the blazing sun. I finally had enough."

"It's quite a change from cooler climates."

"New York gets hot in the summer too. I just don't sit outside in it."

"I hear you," Buck answered. "I'm dive master here, so I'm in the water most of the time."

"Must be nice. I'm hoping to get in some diving while I'm here."

"You dived long?"

"I was in the service a million years ago. Been forever since I was in the water even. Lousy city. Brought all my old equipment." He smiled ruefully. "Took one look in your dive shop and realized I was lugging around a bunch of junk."

"I was in the teams too," Buck told him. "Got my dream job here." He shook his head. "You don't want to be diving with antique equipment—it's risking your life. We'll fix you up with something in the dive shop, no problem."

"Great," the man sipped his drink. "Charlie." He held out his hand.

"Buck."

Henry looked up, realizing they were waiting for his response. "Henry. I'm Henry."

"You work here too?"

"Nope, got a place on the far end of the island. Just a beach bum," he looked into his glass.

"Nice life if you can get it." Charlie looked down. "That your pig?"

"Yep," Henry answered monosyllabically.

"Huh," Charlie turned back to Buck. "So what sort of dives do you have?"

"Well, the new reef is the closest. Quite a lot to see there."

"Yeah, you guys sunk a ship or something to build it?"

"We sure did," Buck said proudly. "It's something to see. There's a lot of corals and fish there already on the island side."

Charlie savored a swallow of his punch, his muscular arm bulging from his polo shirt. "So you mostly dive the island side?"

"Yeah, the other side's for the scientists to research. More dangerous currents there, truth to tell. Some of the tourists aren't used to that, so we stick to the island side. If you want deep dives, there's a terrific reef about a mile offshore. Lots to see there. We run regular trips."

"That sounds great. I'll take the wife to the shallows—she's not really a diver—and go on a real dive later."

"Sign up at the concierge desk." Buck drained his glass and stood up, patting the slumbering pig. "I'll make sure you see some stuff."

"Looking forward to it." Charlie took out his phone.

After sitting out on the hot sand beach, Mia decided to walk to the spa on the shady paths through the palm trees. She peeked in the bar as she went through the hotel. Henry sat, still shirtless, hat politely on the stool next to him, with his pig sprawled out under his feet, contentedly snuffling in her sleep. Her nose was pink and her sparse, but healthy looking coat had black spots on a pinky white background. The barman ignored the pig, but Mia noticed a cool dish of water thoughtfully placed by the animal's side. Guests were pointing and smiling at the animal. As she watched, a woman leaned down for a photo with the little pig.

Mia noted it was an open air bar, with storm shutters flung wide open to the elements. She couldn't exactly smell the pig, but she could still smell the idea of a pig. She only hoped Henry didn't patronize the main dining room with his companion. She—or the health inspector—would have to put a foot down then.

Very few guests were out and about under the dappled shade of the palm trees. One elderly man happily snored in a hammock, panama hat tipped over his face. An older woman lazed on a blue striped blanket piled high with pillows, leisurely reading on the lawn. Most people not on the beach or off on an adventure were probably taking an afternoon nap inside during the hottest part of the day.

The spa building was deceptively large. At first glance, it appeared a cute little private salon with its chalkboard "menu" and discrete hand painted sign. Mia opened the blue wood door and entered another world, one designed for sensual luxury.

The building wrapped around a large open courtyard, ringed by shaded verandas and billowing white curtains shielding guests from the sun and onlookers during their treatments. A long pool stretched the length of the courtyard, with a smooth waterfall sheet flowing from polished limestone. Several women relaxed on the shallow pool stairs, gossiping with extravagant gestures. Potted palm trees, in varied shades of bright blue ceramic planters, were spaced around the courtyard, adding a tropical touch of green leaves.

"Ms. Mia, it's good to have you back on the island." The receptionist smiled up at her in friendly recognition.

"Thanks, Sheila, I'm glad to be back. And I'm certainly ready for a relaxing massage today."

The bright eyed young woman looked down at her schedule, sweeping her hair behind her ear. "Just a massage, Ms. Mia?" She added with an enticing smile, "Are you sure I can't tempt you to a facial, as well?"

Mia laughed. "You can probably tempt me sometime this week. I want to leave in time to rest a little before dinner."

Sheila nodded, long beaded earring swinging with the motion. "I totally understand." She rose, ushering Mia past the serene blue pool, out of the courtyard and down a long dock floating over the turquoise blue water. Four shingled huts perched at the very end of the dock.

Opening a door in the far right hut, Sheila guided Mia inside the little building, "Enjoy!"

Ruth waited for her, holding out a fluffy robe. "Hi, Ms. Mia. Good to see you again. Just you change and I'll be right back," she instructed with a beatific smile.

The small whitewashed hut was open to the ocean side with a view out to blue infinity. Half the floor underneath was glass, showing curious fish and beautiful coral reefs below. As she watched, a bright blue angelfish darted under her feet, hiding in their shadow. Mia laughed. "I do love this view!"

"Isn't it wonderful?" Ruth said, her softly rounded arms working briskly, mixing a sweet smelling oil with the assurance of a master chemist. "I love working out here, nice breeze all the time and the ocean everywhere. You wouldn't believe the animals I've seen through this floor. One time, a baby dolphin stayed there, just looking at me through the glass, for the longest time. I swear that cutie was smiling at me." She shook her head in wonderment. "Now, Ms. Mia, are you looking for calm and relaxing—or just a touch of pep?"

"Oh, I think total relaxation this afternoon," Mia's jangled nerves still needed a little calming.

"I'm using babassu oil today, with seaweed—very nourishing to the skin, seaweed—and some passion fruit oil for calming down inflammation. I gather the seaweed myself on the island. The most wonderful old woman makes the passion fruit oil—George's old grandmama." Ruth laughed. "She's well past ninety and has the most beautiful skin you've ever seen. Barely a wrinkle and she swears by her passion fruit. Says it'll cure any skin issues."

"That's worth a try, then," Mia laughed. "She ought to know."

Ruth put the finishing touches to her masterpiece, and held it under Mia's face. "Now, doesn't that smell lovely?" The bright aroma of the passion fruit melded perfectly with the salt of the seaweed.

"Ambrosial." Mia lay down, her head cradled in a sublime view of the ocean floor below. "The reef's grown up so much since we built this," she said as she noticed a beautiful pinky purple sea fan. "It was mostly bare sand a few years ago. Just a few remnants of reef left."

"It gets more interesting all the time," Ruth told her. "Every week I see a new fish." She pointed to a fat field guide on her table. "I keep that near to learn their names."

As Ruth began the massage, Mia felt herself ease into the table as Ruth kneaded her muscles with the luxurious oils melting into her skin. Watched bright fish swim by, she relaxed into the experience. "My goodness, Ruth, I didn't realize I was still so tense after yoga this morning. I really needed this."

"Sounds like you have reason to be," Ruth suggested diffidently. "That was bad trouble you had this morning. Make anyone tense." Her hands kneaded and soothed knots.

"So you've heard about that, then?"

"Of course, no secrets on an island this small," Ruth sounded surprised that Mia would ask. Her necklace of beads clacked soothingly as she worked out a difficult muscle. A princess parrotfish, striped with bright blues and pinks, and just a dash of yellow, swam slowly by under Mia, sunlight sparkling on its scales.

"You know I'm looking for a man that was lying on the beach this morning?"

"A bearded man," Ruth added. "Yes, Ms. Mia."

"George suggested it could possibly be your former boyfriend, Robert."

Ruth paused a beat in her massage. "No, I don't think so, Ms. Mia," she concluded after due deliberation, restarting her kneading.

"No?"

"Well, Robert had a long beard, kind of dirty gray. Never shaved that I saw."

"Maybe he cut it short?" Mia suggested.

"Still wouldn't be dark, would it, then?" Ruth said with decision. "And last I heard, he was creeping on some other woman. The boys made it no fun to get to me."

"Good for them."

"Lots of trouble to pay for gas to out here, to see a woman who don't want to see you. Not much fun when the men throw you off the island." She shrugged. "I think he just came that extra time or two to prove he could get away with it, that they couldn't stop him. Some men are like that." Her tone was final. She kneaded Mia's shoulders firmly to emphasize her point.

"I think you're probably right, Ruth," Mia agreed. "I hope your next boyfriend is better."

Ruth chuckled, "Oh, I found me a better one, right here on the island. He treats me right."

"Good, you deserve it."

After the massage, Mia, tenderly enveloped in a fluffy white robe, made her way to the little landing between the huts, perched on the edge of the ocean, chairs suspended on glass. She curled up, leaning over the arm of the chair, and watched the fish darting like bright gems between the corals below.

"It's wonderful, isn't it?" an abrupt voice startled her. A white robe wrapped Amy Smith padded to the lounge chair beside Mia, positioning herself for a view of the reef below. "I could get used to this." She shifted her weight slightly, tucking her robe around her sturdy legs. "I guess I soon will," she laughed softly to herself. "My life is definitely changing for the better soon." Her smile widened, with a little curve on one side, gleeful at the upcoming shift in her fortune. Her bare foot tapped the glass.

"How nice," Mia told her. "Are you changing jobs?" she asked curiously. Or divorcing, she thought to herself, thinking of Amy's interactions with her husband.

Amy chuckled a little, "Even better. I'm retiring soon."

"Very nice, indeed," Mia said. "You're lucky to be able to retire so young."

"Life's about making your own luck," Amy rejoined. "Ooh, look at that school!" A vivid blue school of chromis darted around a rock, then skirted warily past an anemone.

"Lovely," Mia agreed. "Do you dive, or just your husband?"

"My husband?" Amy tucked the robe neck closer. "Oh, that's right, you saved me when he dumped that load of gear on me." She grimaced and slicked her wet hair back. "I'd like to, but I've just taken a few scuba lessons. I got busy at work and didn't have time to finish."

"You could finish training here," Mia suggested. "There's a beginner's class."

"Maybe," Amy hesitated. "I don't know if I'll have time this trip."

"If you're retiring soon, that would be a fun thing to learn. There are so many interesting places to dive around the world and they all have their special moments."

Amy nodded, clearly preferring that option. "That sounds like a plan."

"Oh, look at that trunkfish with all the spots," Mia pointed. "Adorable."

Amy leaned back into her lounge chair, looking out into infinity. Her mind swam with future plans. Retirement, not just to some lousy cramped apartment, scrimping and saving to make ends meet. Not her. Not anymore. She'd be living this life full time, in fancy hotels at exotic locations, eating gourmet meals prepared by big name chefs. Afternoons spent like this, having an expert masseuse work the kinks out of her back, surrounded by freaking paradise. She tested her shoulders, enjoying their newly supple movement. Only the rich felt this kind of ease in life.

She was tired of her boss ordering her around, keeping her down. Her credit card bill hurt every time she looked at it. She'd barely seen her apartment at all last year, but still had to pay a fortune to keep it.

Amy looked around her at the frosty glass on the table, the luxurious white robe, the plump cushions of the lounge chair. This was a far cry from the crowded neighborhood spa, brimmed with screeching voices, a massage to the sound of nearby blow dryers, she'd "treated" herself to on her last birthday. She shuddered and surveyed the calm, turquoise water. This was the life, the life she was meant to live.

Only her partner was going to be a problem. Him and his stupid junk dive equipment. She was tired of him, sick of seeing him sneering at her choice of books, what she ordered for dinner, ordering her around, making her do everything herself, and laughing at her all the time, like she didn't know it. She couldn't wait to get rid of him.

Only she needed him to make this work. More than he needed her, to tell the truth. She planned future scenarios, unable to think of a way she could be finished with him quite yet. She'd have to wait it out, let him think she was still in lock step with him. Then, as soon as she could, she'd be done with him. And good riddance.

Her mind drifted, floating away on fluffy white clouds, building castles in the air.

Mia meandered back to her cottage by the back service paths, peaceful under the lengthening purple shadows of the palm trees. She walked slowly, enjoying the renewed ease of her stride after the massage. She looked forward to the next few weeks on the island. If only she hadn't seen that body this morning, paradise would be perfect.

Smiling in greeting, Mia moved out of the way of a housekeeper trundling a large linens cart. The woman ambled along the path at a leisurely, but steady pace. Nodding to Mia, she slowed to a halt and hesitatingly asked, "Ms. Mia?" Her shy smile was uncertain.

"Yes, Sandy?" Mia said, reading her name tag. "I don't think we've met before." She asked suddenly, with a warm smile, "You're George's special friend, aren't you? He's a good man, that one."

"Yes, ma'am," Sandy's cheeks reddened and she ducked her head down shyly. "George said you were looking for anything odd with the guests? Something to do with the well check where we couldn't find anyone looking hurt?"

"That's right, Sandy. Can you think of anything?"

"Well, there was something odd. I don't know if it's what you want to know, but," she looked at Mia for guidance.

"Anything odd might explain it, Sandy. Please go on."

Sandy's words came out in a rush, "That man who doesn't have real dive gear, Mr. Smith. Mr. Charlie Smith. George said he told you what I said earlier," she looked at Mia for confirmation. "Mr. Smith was in Mr. Wilson's cottage this morning. The messy rich kids with all the computers. No broughtupsy, those ones," she clarified, putting one hand on a curvaceous hip.

"Really? What was he doing there?"

"Well, I was cleaning, you see. They stopped talking when I came through the room." Sandy shrugged a little, "I didn't know you wanted us to look for anything going on then, so I wasn't listening specially. Just couldn't help overhearing them while I was cleaning."

Mia nodded in understanding.

"Mr. Wilson was very upset, throwing stuff around and cursing. Making a big mess. Told Mr. Smith he got him into this, he'd have to get him out. Mr. Smith was trying to reassure him. I thought it was strange, you know. To be arguing like that."

"Very interesting," Mia agreed.

"I didn't know anything was wrong then, or I would have listened better," Sandy assured Mia. "I usually don't pay attention to what the guests talk about. I was just surprised they knew each other."

"I am too," Mia said. "They certainly didn't look like they were friends or even acquainted on the beach, just now."

"That's why I thought you'd like to know. It's odd," Sandy told her. With a sudden gush, she reassured Mia, "Ms. Mia, we think, most of us, that is, you really saw that bearded man on the beach, just like you said. There's something not right on the island. It doesn't feel right with the last guests that come. Like someone's real angry or upset, you know," She shivered a little, strong shoulders moving supplely beneath her crisp uniform.

"George says you always fix things up when you come to the island. I know you'll fix this."

Mia didn't know what to say about Sandy's confidence in her. "Why, thank you, Sandy." She felt thankful someone believed her and had been kind enough to tell her so.

"We're looking hard for the missing man in our spare time. We, all of us that believe you saw him. We know you weren't just seeing things like some say. We'll find him for you if he's on the island." She squared her small, firm chin, warm brown eyes gazed at Mia with concern.

Mia coughed a little, her eyes tearing up at Sandy's statement. "Thank you. I don't think I was seeing things either." She looked directly into Sandy's clear, bright eyes. "I just don't know what happened after that yet."

"We'll find him for you if he's on the island still, don't you worry." She smiled wholeheartedly at Mia, her words ringing true.

"Sandy, I don't know what to say. That means a lot to me." Mia blinked rapidly a few times and coughed slightly. "I did have one potential idea. May I run it by you?"

"Yes, ma'am," Sandy's eyes were eager.

"Could the man on the beach have been a guest who was supposed to leave yesterday, perhaps?"

Sandy squinched up her face, thinking hard. "It's possible, I guess." She shrugged, "People check in and out of the front desk. No one checks to see if they got on the boat like they were supposed to. If they're not in their rooms, we assume they've left. Nowhere to get food on the island, anyhow, without a room, unless you work here. Of course, a guest could have brought extra food with them," she added, considering the idea.

"Do you remember if any departing guests had beards?"

"I can't think of a one," Sandy paused a beat in thought. "I can ask around for you, if you'd like. Housekeeping doesn't come in contact with guests as much as some of the other crew. Mostly I try to clean while guests aren't in their rooms. Better for everyone."

"That's true," Mia agreed. "I'd really appreciate it, Sandy."

"No problem," Sandy said. "Still, Ms. Mia, there's a big question we have." She spread her hands wide, sparkly nail polish glittering in the sunlight. "What happened to that man right after you saw him?"

"I don't know, Sandy. It's a good question."

Sandy smoothly wheeled her jingling cart down the path, mulling over where the missing man might be hiding. He wasn't in one of the rooms, that she knew. Housekeeping cleaned too well for any dust to be hidden under the bed, let alone a man.

He could have shaved that beard and disappeared into the rest of the guests, if he was still alive. Sandy shook her head and opened the door of the next room on her schedule, avoiding unpleasant surprises for her and her guests by calling out in a ringing voice, "Housekeeping!" No guests here, just an unmade bed and a bathroom needing a wipe down. She moved unhurriedly through the room, leaving order in her wake, while her mind focused on the problem of the missing man.

Something was off about the island today, that was for sure. The crew were all on edge, snapping a little, complaining about things they'd never bother about usually. Ms. Mia had seen a dead man and the whole island knew it. But where did the man go? It felt like waiting for a storm to break, where you could see distant lightning. She didn't really believe in ghosts, but if she did, she'd say this heavy unease of the island was his ghost unable to rest, haunting the island until his body was properly buried. She shivered a little as a cloud shadowed the bright sun.

If a dead man disappeared off a beach, someone got him off that beach. Dead men don't walk, except in the spirit world.

Herself, if she had a dead body to get rid of, she'd dump him far out to sea. But none of the big boats had been that far out. Just small skiffs, like Chef Louis's. You couldn't hide a conch shell in one of those, let alone a man's body. To know tonight's menu, you could check out the chef's boat as he docked. No one could have dumped a body out at sea without everyone seeing it leave, if you took a skiff. Not that Chef Louis or anyone else she knew would kill anyone.

Sandy knew the groundskeepers had been searching the hotel grounds for a body, but up in the blackwater hammocks, there were plenty of places to hide a body. Especially if you didn't care particularly what happened to it afterwards. She screwed up her face in disgust and gave the shining mirror a final polish with extra gusto.

It'd be hard to haul a body through the hotel grounds without someone noticing. Even late at night, you'd get security guards and guests taking late night strolls when their time zones were off. It'd be taking a big risk to carry a body out in the open. Of course, it'd be worth any risk to get rid of the body, if you were a murderer.

Sandy closed the door and trundled her cart along to the next cottage. George, she smiled to herself at his vehement defense of Ms. Mia in the hospitality team lounge, wholeheartedly believed Ms. Mia. So she did too. George knew people, better than she did usually. She liked to believe the best about everyone, but unfortunately people didn't always do their best.

She opened the last cottage door and sighed heavily. This Skip Wilson was a pig. No, pigs, she thought, were much cleaner. Nicer, too. Getting a trash bag out, she started picking up paper and empty candy wrappers. Remembering how he'd yelled at her yesterday for moving his game setup on the coffee table, she carefully wiped around the equipment and placed the pile of dirty dishes outside the door for the busboy to collect.

She opened the large French doors wide, letting fresh air flood through the stuffy room. "Let's get some air in this room. It's surprising they don't asphyxiate in this place," she said to herself. Spraying a sweet smelling citrus cleaner with abandon, she wiped down the little kitchen briskly. Grabbing clean sheets from her cart, she opened the bedroom door. A man loomed up, his dark shape suddenly filling the doorway. She screamed, dropping the sheets and turning to run.

"Hey, sorry, sorry," he quickly called out. "Didn't mean to scare you." He moved fast, starting to block her way, then hanging back a little. "Really, I'm so sorry I scared you," he reassured her.

Sandy turned slightly, recognizing the guest, Mr. Smith, staying with his wife in one of the double rooms. She continued backing toward the door, moving away warily, as if in a room with an unexpected tiger. Some guests could turn ugly, and this man didn't belong in this room.

"I'm sorry. I didn't hear you come in," he said, soothing voice silky smooth. "I'd have called out, told you I was here." He held his bare hands out in supplication, emphasizing he held no weapon.

She stopped, but didn't come closer. "This isn't your room," she accused.

"No, no, it's Skip Wilson's. Skip Wilson's room," he repeated. "I'm just grabbing some papers he needed, that's all. We're in a meeting. He gave me the key," he held out his hand with the key card in it confidently. "See?"

Sandy frowned. "How do I know that's not your room key?"

He laughed loud and his mouth widened, but his sharp eyes stayed steady on hers, unblinking. "I'm in here, aren't I?" He moved his square shoulders deprecatingly.

"I guess," Sandy agreed hesitantly. She moved back toward her cart, feeling off balance and wanting to leave. She could always finish the bedrooms later. She didn't want to be alone in the cottage with this man. "I don't want to bother you, then."

"No worries, I'm just leaving." Mr. Smith sauntered out with a smooth, cocky stride, carrying a few papers, leaving Sandy uncertain whether he'd been there with Skip Wilson's knowledge or not. She'd seen him meeting with Mr. Wilson that morning, so it was probably okay.

She shrugged, deciding it wasn't her concern since he'd obviously had a key card, and began changing the rumpled sheets. What a mess they'd left.

Walking on the rambling path to her cottage, Mia wondered the same thing. Whether the man was alive or dead, he had to be somewhere. He hadn't disappeared in a cloud of smoke, after all.

If the entire island knew she'd seen a man on the beach this morning, which it appeared they did, it was just a matter of time before Mark heard all about it—if Buck hadn't already informed him of his stepmother's mental breakdown. A lot of people were actively trying to help her, even if it did sound like perhaps they'd taken sides for and against her seeing imaginary dead bodies. She wondered what the resort team's betting odds on her sanity were. Or her seeing another dead body.

Frowning, her mouth drooped a little, then her lips tightened in a determined line. She had to find the man she'd seen before things got extremely awkward, or her family decided to descend on her. There was nothing more annoying than a concerned, solicitous family when you were trying to accomplish something they thought hazardous.

Would a dead body be easier or more difficult to hide than an injured man?

An injured man, particularly if you wanted him to recover, would be almost impossible to hide on an island this size. The guest rooms had been searched. The hospitality team and their families were in and out of each other's homes all day, from what she remembered. It would be very unusual to have windows shuttered and doors closed, except during a storm. People simply didn't lock up on the island. There was no crime in the tight knit community, so no need for locked doors.

While there were wildlife areas with heavy undergrowth, there weren't unused buildings scattered around the island, nowhere under cover an injured man could heal. The hotel was fully booked. Even if the beard had been shaved, a sick man would be impossible to hide.

But a dead man? A dead man could easily be hidden in all sorts of places, from under supplies in a landscaping shed to a clump of bushes. She poked around a neat stack of concrete blocks, next to a half built shed. No obvious dead bodies here, but there were potential hiding spots all over the island.

Until the body began to smell, that is. Then, someone would certainly notice it. She wrinkled her nose.

So there had to be a plan to get the body off the island.

If Mia was stuck with a dead body to dispose of on a small island, the first thing she would look for was boat access. A limited amount of guests brought their own boats, but boats were also available for dive outings or fishing. Of course, carrying a body out to a boat docked at the marina would probably be noticed. A smaller craft might pull up on the beach, like the trespasser Robert had. Or you might take your chances moving it very early in the morning, like when she'd found the body.

She should look into the boats next.

With that decision made, she walked up the steps of her charming cottage, considering her dinner plans.

Dinner on the island called for only slightly more formal attire than daytime, and the dress code was mostly the guest's choice. While flip flops and t-shirts were not allowed in the main restaurant, guests might show up in almost anything else. But Mia adored the ritual of dressing up to dine well.

For her first festive dinner on the island, she decided on a pale blue fitted sheath coming to just below her knees, embroidered around the neckline and waist with gold and deep blue flowers. She carefully lined her upper eyelids with a warm brown, then smudged the edges, adding mascara for a touch more definition. She smoothed pink lipstick over her lips and chose deep blue spinel earrings, given to her by her husband to celebrate the opening festivities of this very hotel. Smiling at herself in the mirror, she almost saw Leo smiling back over her shoulder, as he so often had. Swirling a gossamer blue wrap around her shoulders, she walked down the path to the restaurant.

While the night air wasn't exactly chilly, it was much cooler than the day, so she was glad of the wrap as she walked to the restaurant. The hotel's more formal restaurant, Fritters, was across from the main hotel building, overlooking the choppier, rocky shore of the island with large picture windows (protected by quickly positioned storm shutters.) The view of the vast Atlantic was spectacular, rolling waves softly crashing on the limestone rock of the island, with nothing but the deep blue of the ocean as far as the eye could see.

Warm white wood panels covered the walls, intensified by dark mahogany floors. Silver glittered in the warm candlelight. White linen draped tablecloths were topped with tiny vases of exotic tropical flowers by each place, along with a flock of crystal wine glasses. Demure wing chairs surrounding the tables were elegantly backed with dark wood, but rich petrol blue damask made for luxurious seating.

George, the headwaiter, tonight wearing a crisp white shirt and tailored black pants, ushered her to a table for three with a full view of the restaurant activity. "Good evening, Ms. Mia," he told her. "Ms. Evie and Buck will be along shortly."

Mia smiled at the little spray of yellow bells by her seat. "Thank you, George." She smiled up at him. "I met Sandy earlier. She's just a lovely woman, isn't she?"

The tips of George's ears reddened. "I certainly think so."

"You need to hold on to that one. She's quite a catch."

"Um," George muttered, his blush growing deeper on his dark skin. He suddenly looked very young and awkward. "Um, what would you like to drink tonight?" He consciously straightened his posture back into that of the perfect headwaiter. "Or shall I send our sommelier over?"

"I'll start with champagne, please. Pierre Gimonnet & Fils Champagne, 2015, I think. Does that work with the feast you've planned?"

"Very good," George approved. "Nice notes of saline and citrus. Would you like something while you're waiting?"

"Yes, please. I'd love to sample a few appetizers."

George nodded and strode off, pausing by Skip Wilson's table to deferentially ask if they needed anything. Skip leaned back in his chair, slouching into the cushioned back. He barely met restaurant rules with a bleach splotched polo shirt. It did have a collar, but Mia was pretty sure it also had holes. He'd pulled a nearby chair up to prop his feet on it. She frowned. Skip was certainly not the kind of guest she preferred staying at her hotels.

The security guard was dining with the little group. They must be old friends, Mia thought, which would explain such an obviously untrained guard taking part in events. He mirrored Skip's every action, from laughing at his jokes to propping his dirty feet on a chair.

Mia remembered Skip's social media company had only risen to its present dizzy heights in the past year or two. She guessed his companions were old college roommates or some such. While they were all obviously uncouth, Skip keeping old friends showed more of a sense of loyalty than she would have guessed from what her daughter had said about The Blare Community.

The helicopter pilot, his injured foot propped on a stool hospitality had brought him, drank his wine steadily, clearly determined to make the most of the occasion. His expression and quickly finger combed hair said he was in a fair amount of pain and self medicating to the limit. Mia hoped he wasn't mixing pain pills and alcohol, but she was certain he was, from his bleary eyes.

Carol sat determinedly upright, obviously ignoring her employer's crudities. She wasn't taking part in the loud guffawing boys' club around the table, but gazed out the window at the rolling waves of the ocean and savored her meal with evident pleasure.

Mia wondered what surprises George had for her tonight. She looked up to see Buck and Evie entering the restaurant and motioned them over. "This view is even more beautiful than my memory. What a beautiful restaurant setting!"

"The meal will be better too," Evie assured her. "Chef Louis is constantly improving his menus. He's an artist, constantly adding little touches."

"Lots of local, seasonal stuff. Most mornings, he runs over to the mainland and raids the markets. He's got it where the fisherman save the very best of their catch for him, and the farmers grow whatever crazy herb he asks them to. Makes for some damn good meals," Buck put in appreciatively.

"He always has a new, seasonal creation," Evie sighed dreamily, her ample curves shifting under her loose, cobalt blue dress. "Always something delicious the guests are raving about. All I have to do is let the artist create."

"I can't wait to try all of them," Mia said. "I'm having a lovely vacation so far, despite that little setback this morning." She smiled ruefully. "Yoga on the beach—Julie is a wonder—then I went to the spa this afternoon and Ruth gave me a marvelous massage. Incredibly relaxing, with the fish swimming beneath the table. I do love that setting." She sipped her champagne, enjoying the subtle pop of the cold bubbles on her tongue.

"That's good, good. A good start to a vacation," Evie replied, but her soft brown eyes were concerned.

Fortunately, George whisked their appetizers before them with a proud smile. Mia was pleased to see more of the delicate conch fritters she'd enjoyed at lunch, but was also interested in sampling new tidbits. She bit into a delicate rice paper roll with just caught tuna and creamy avocado. "Heavenly, George," she enthused.

He beamed at her, then hurried off, probably before she could quiz him more about his romantic intentions with Sandy. Of course, Mia knew now wasn't the time to examine George's love life, not with Evie and Buck here. She would never dream of doing such a thing. Instead, she'd have a nice little chat with George on his own later, make sure he was working up to a ring for Sandy. It was time he settled down and started a family.

Mia did so like to see people happy. Sometimes they just needed a tiny nudge in the right direction, which she was always happy to provide for her dear friends.

Glancing at Buck's lined face, she considered whether it was too soon for him to start dating again and decided, with a little disappointment, that it was. He needed more time to mourn Sarah. Mia wasn't over the shock of Sarah's sudden death, so he certainly wasn't yet. That was all right—it would give her plenty of time to find just the right woman for him. Buck deserved someone very special, indeed.

Suddenly, she realized Buck had asked her something and was evidently waiting for a response, his face concerned. "I'm sorry, I was just enjoying this scrumptious tuna roll. Could you please repeat that?"

He cleared his throat and tried again, brow furrows deepening. "I wondered if you felt up to going for a dive tomorrow afternoon? I have a private lesson slot open." He added, "There's no rush. We can always go next week." His knee jiggled under the table, just in Mia's line of vision.

"Tomorrow sounds perfect," Mia told him with pleasure. "Sign me up."

Buck nodded, his forehead smoothing. "The reef's changed a lot since you were here last."

"I haven't been diving since then," Mia confessed. She twisted her lips to the side, looking out at the vast ocean. "It was just something Leo and I did together, you know?"

"I know," Buck told her gently, his sharp blue eyes softening as he looked at her, then looked down at his place setting, fiddling with the reflections on his knife. "Leo did love diving. I think he tried to buy as many hotels in dive spots as possible." He barked a quick laugh.

She smiled back,"I know he did." Mia coughed a little and looked around the room. She observed, her voice a little choked up, "Quite a full house we have, Evie."

"Isn't it great? That travel site mentioning us as a hidden getaway really filled up our empty slots." Evie looked with pride around the full dining room. "Nicole really did well with getting that through."

"I'm proud of her," Mia said. Her daughter was very good at getting the right influencers into the right hotels.

Everyone around her seemed pleased with their dining experience, from what Mia could see. Mr. and Mrs. Smith had scored one of the tables by the huge windows and, if not exactly deep in conversation with each other, were alternating their satisfied attention between the view and the food. Two obvious honeymooners at the table beside them sat with entwined hands, gazing into each other's eyes, oblivious of the food and view. Mia sighed with nostalgia. A loved one's eyes were the most beautiful thing to see in the world. No view, no matter how sublime, could compete.

The recent divorcée, Megan, sat alone in the middle of the room, foot impatiently tapping, waiting for her dinner to be served. She was dressed in a daring backless dress, her knobbly spine rimmed with tiny rows of green sequins. With a hungry look, she checked out every male who came into the room. Mia supposed that eventually she would find someone, but a romantic restaurant filled with couples was certainly not the best place to start.

Or maybe it was. On his next off color joke, Megan joined in with Skip's loud laughter, deliberately catching his eye. He smiled broader, winking at her.

Carol frowned, clearly catching the exchange. She looked out the window, obviously determined to ignore her dinner group and enjoy the rest of the experience.

Surveying the mouthwatering appetizers before her, Mia thoughtfully took a spoonful of the conch ceviche. Tangy, but not overwhelmed by lime juice, the crunch of fresh cucumber and chewy conch melded into a luscious combination.

The retired Rodriguezes, Donna and Todd, she reminded herself, weren't next to the window view, but at a table against the far wall. Donna was chattering happily and Todd merely nodded along, enjoying the sparkling happiness on his wife's face. Their plates came and Mia could almost hear the oohs and ahhs from across the room.

"They seem happy," Mia nodded discretely. "Nice couple, she was in my yoga class."

"They went diving with me this afternoon," Buck told her. "He was pretty good, I'd guess some military training in his youth, but she needed a lot of help for her first go." Buck screwed up his face in annoyance. "He wandered off by himself—like I constantly tell everyone not to do—exploring the far side of the reef. I had to practically put out a search party for him. He turned up suddenly when his air hit fifty psi." He shook his head. "If people would just follow the rules, life would be so much simpler."

Evie laughed, "They never will."

"Nope," Buck agreed. "It's like they're trying to get themselves killed." His eyes met Mia's and skittered off.

"I promise not to wander off while diving," Mia said gently.

"No, I know you won't."

Mia took a bite of her conch fritter. Perfectly crispy outside and delicately creamy inside.

Guffaws of laughter rang through the room. Startled, everyone stared at Skip's table. Skip slapped the table, making the glasses jump, and tears of laughter ran down his face. Carol, her face showing her distaste of whatever the joke was, deliberately shoved her chair back and left the table, walking with a straight flat back out of the restaurant. The three men ignored her and huddled closer, repeating their raucous laughter.

With a broad sweep of his arm, Skip motioned Megan over to take Carol's place. She swung her slim hips seductively beneath the sparkling dress as she changed tables, joining in the loud laughter with a flirtatious high pitched giggle, leaning in to the group.

"I really don't understand why they're here," Evie said, her lips pursing in distaste. "It certainly doesn't seem like their sort of hotel." She sat back in her comfortable chair, pretending not to stare at the obnoxious group.

"The reef," Mia suggested. "It's really the most private reef around, at least where you still have a hotel to stay at instead of a private house. The others you have to moor a boat to spend serious dive time on."

Buck objected, "They haven't even been to the reef. No reservations to go, either." He shrugged. "I checked up, so I could be their dive master. Not leave them with one of the kids." He glanced at Skip's group, nostrils pinching in distaste. "Both because he's VIP— and for safety. If anyone wouldn't follow safety instructions, it's that lot."

"It's still their first full day," Evie demurred. Her expression changed, "Look, here's George with our meal."

All of their attention was immediately taken by the bounty of George's main course. For Mia, he had a rich fish stew, spicy and tomato filled, but replete with delicate pieces of white fish and topped by clams. Buck was presented with a seared tuna steak, still deep red on the inside. He happily squeezed a lemon onto it, commenting, "This job really is the best."

Evie received a seed encrusted snapper, fresh from the ocean. Silence and the soft clinks of silverware reigned at their table.

Dessert was delicious, passionfruit ice cream with caramel sauce drizzled on it. Mia savored each spoonful slowly, enjoying the tart bite of the passionfruit with the rich sweetness of the caramel.

"That was a feast," she said after the last spoonful.

"George always does know what to bring," Evie said with a sigh.

"He always knows the best stuff going in the kitchen," Buck agreed with a satisfied smile. Then, he straightened in his soft chair and exchanged a quick glance with Evie, who placed her elbows on the table and leaned forward, frowning.

Mia inwardly sighed.

"Look, Mia, we need to have a little talk with you," Buck stated, swiping a worried hand across his hair. "We're worried about you."

"I know you've been talking to my team behind my back," Evie said. She fiddled with her dessert fork, twisting it around. "It's upsetting everyone."

"Is it?" Mia had yet to meet resort team members who seemed remotely upset by her questions.

"Of course it is," Evie remonstrated, pulling her round figure up in the chair. Then she sighed and slumped back, holding out her hands in protest, "Look, I believed you. We did the health check like you asked. It's like you think I didn't do a good job on that." Her full lips puckered.

Mia reassured her, "Of course you did a good job, Evie. You're always very efficient."

"Then why the blazes—" Buck paused and restarted, "Why are you still asking so many questions about a bearded man?"

"Because I saw a dead bearded man lying on the beach," Mia said simply.

"But you didn't," Buck stated. "There's no such man on the island." He looked at Evie. "Didn't you trust Evie and I to check?" His blue eyes looked steadily into hers.

"I did," Mia told him. "But while neither of you might believe me, I refuse to doubt the evidence of my own eyes, so I'm looking for an explanation for what I saw." She rose. "I'm going back to my cottage now. Good night."

"But, Mia...," Buck said weakly.

"Don't leave like this," Evie urged, brown eyes soft. "We care about you, Mia."

"I know you do. That's why I'm leaving now," Mia replied firmly. She briskly left the restaurant to discordant peals of laughter from Skip's table.

Buck and Evie looked at each other after Mia had walked off. Evie said hesitatingly, "Is there any way Mia could have seen," she looked around, lowering her voice, "what she thought she saw?"

Buck shook his head sadly. "I can't think of anything she could have even mistaken for a dead man. She's been stressed and just," he shifted uncomfortably in the soft chair, "saw things. People do some weird things under stress." He shook his head.

"Should we call Mark?" Evie asked, clearly not wanting to. "Or maybe Nicole? She might handle her mom better."

"Let Mia sleep on it, see if she feels differently in the morning," Buck told her. "I'll have a serious talk with her after our dive tomorrow, when she's relaxed a bit. I'm guessing with a good night's sleep, she'll be a little more reasonable. I don't want to get her back up about it." He grinned halfheartedly. "You know how stubborn she can be."

"I don't know—her family would want to know." Evie turned her glass on the table, watching the amber glow of the wine shimmer.

"Just until tomorrow afternoon, not long," Buck said. "It'll be a heck of a lot easier to tell them the problem is over and done with, than to tell them Mia is seeing things." He ran a hand across his close cropped silver hair.

"I guess." Evie toyed with her spoon, scooping up a last mouthful of caramel. "Dinner was good. I'd eat more, but I'm stuffed." She patted her belly, ample curves shifting under her loose dress.

"Yeah, it's dangerous having a restaurant this good on site," Buck agreed. He looked quizzically at Evie. "So why don't I ever see you here with Henry?"

"Henry?" Evie moved her spoon around, not finding any more caramel. "Why would I bring Henry here?"

"You bring him food from this place, right?" There wasn't much Buck didn't know about this island.

Evie blushed, round cheeks rosy. "Well, sometimes." She shifted her gaze across the restaurant, then back at her spoon, her usual confident spirit depressed. "He doesn't take proper care of himself. The man has to eat." She added defiantly, "Not like there're a lot of restaurants on the island."

"He's a good man, Evie. Been through a lot," Buck added in a soothing tone.

"I know he has." Her luminous brown eyes looked at him seriously. "Look, I don't want to start anything." She shook her head. "Just let it lie, Buck. Mia's enough to deal with right now."

"Sure, Evie." He looked at his empty plate as if he could have his dessert magically reappear. "You think George would give us seconds on dessert?"

Mia felt upset and on edge after Buck and Evie's unwanted intervention. She headed down to the beach, walking along the shore with her shoes in her hand. A full moon silvered the sand, gilding the tops of the waves. She walked far up the beach, past the event center, thinking to herself.

As a reasonable person, she did listen to friends who cared about her. But while she was willing to accept alternate explanations for what she'd seen—the man was injured, it had been a trick—she was not willing to accept that the man had never been there at all, only a figment of her imagination. And with the evidence of the sand disturbance backing her up, Buck shouldn't be asking her not believe the evidence of her own eyes.

Her steps moved slowly through the cold sand, moving aside the small grains with effort, like the effort of slogging through the ephemeral facts in search of small grains of truth. But how? She slowly walked on.

She realized she had gone far past the workshop center and looked at her watch, tiny spinels sparkling in the moonlight. It was far past midnight. She should head back and get a good night's sleep. Sleeping on a problem was often the first step toward a solution.

She returned with a brisker step, slowing with curiosity as she approached the dive dock. Lights shown in the dark water, far out on the reef. They must be doing a night dive. For a few minutes, she watched the green tinged lights moving deep under the waves, looking alien under the moonlight. She wondered why Buck hadn't mentioned the upcoming night dive at dinner. Seeing the reef life at night would be an amazing experience. She'd have to sign up for it tomorrow.

Her mouth twisted a bit at the thought of Buck telling her she was imagining seeing a dead man on the beach. Her teeth gritted at the thought of him being so sweet and understanding about the whole thing, talking about calling her kids and telling them about how she was losing her mind because of stress. Stress, her foot! She would have to put a stop to that immediately.

Tomorrow, she had to find that body.

5

Happy Trails

Mia enjoyed an early breakfast in her cottage, brought to her by the smiling Elizabeth, almost bouncing up the steps in her practical neon colored tennis shoes. "Good morning to you!"

"And to you," Mia returned. "Any news this morning?"

"Nothing to do with that man you saw." Elizabeth shook her head with disappointment, smile briefly dimming, then returning to full wattage. "Just as well, I think, Ms. Mia. I know you saw him like you said, but we don't want the hotel mixed up with any nasty business. Worries the guests and makes them leave. I'm glad he took himself off and isn't bothering us any more.

You can just have a nice day and relax." She placed the tray on the little porch table with a flourish. "See you later, Ms. Mia!"

"Thanks, Elizabeth," Mia returned the wave as Elizabeth ran down the steps, her bright shoes rapidly disappearing around the corner.

She ate a leisurely breakfast, enjoying both the delicious omelet with a papaya on the side and the translucent turquoise waters spread out before her. Palm tree fronds clacked in the slight breeze and small birds chirped in the shrubs below. The smell of exotic flowers stirred in the air as the yellow bells shifted in the gentle breeze. It was a morning to savor, but Mia had work to do.

She had to find that body today, despite Elizabeth's well intentioned advice. If something bad had happened on her island, it was up to her to clean up the mess.

The problem was, from a murderer's point of view, if she had saddled herself with a dead body, the very first thing she would have done on an island would be to take a boat out and dump it in the ocean. No one wanted to hold on to a body. Bodies weren't something you wanted hanging out in your hotel room for any length of time, besides being rather incriminating evidence.

She hadn't seen or heard a boat leave the marina during the time the body had disappeared. And she would have heard an engine in the still morning air. Anything paddled couldn't have disappeared before she returned to the beach since she hadn't been gone for very long. That left two possibilities she could think of.

Dressing quickly in a soft green embroidered tunic, jeweled sandals and natural linen capris, she planned her day. She placed delicate mint green spinel stud earrings in her ears and a soft rose lipstick across her lips. She was ready for battle in paradise now.

Deliberately taking the beach route to the hotel, she barely glanced at the spot she'd seen the body, striding decisively across the smoothly swept sand. She passed by the marina and dive dock, continuing up the beach. Nodding to morning spa guests cocooned in soft white robes, she walked on, looking for signs that a boat had pulled up the beach past high tide and hidden in the lush green plants along the beach edge. Finally, she reached her destination.

She'd remembered Henry used to have a boat pulled up close to his little shack, half hidden in a thatched lean to. She went all the way up to his boat, looking for signs it had recently been in the water. The sand in front of the battered boat was marked by wind, a few footprints and little holes she guessed were made by pig feet. A few palm fronds lay on the sand and a lizard scuttled by, rattling the dry fronds in his rush to get away from the interloper.

"Hey, you!"

Mia looked up into the furiously shaking beard. Not the way she was accustomed to being addressed, but she politely returned, "Hello?"

"What are you doing back there?" Henry accused her, coming out of the open, unpainted doorway. "Why are you messing with my stuff? My home isn't open to tourists." He put his hands on his hips and glared menacingly.

"I was looking at your boat," Mia said truthfully.

His jaw set truculently. "Why? It's my boat, not the hotel's. It's not for rent." He stepped off his porch, coming toward her, his mouth hard and his eyes narrowed to slits. His long, unkempt beard, reached down his chest, but it didn't seem dirty, at least, Mia thought with relief. He was wearing what appeared to be the same cutoffs as yesterday and nothing else but leather tanned skin. "Go rent one on the beach." He waved his hand toward the marina.

His shack had once been a charming vacation cottage on the beach, but neglect had turned the remnants of white paint dirty, with gray wood showing through leprous patches. The wide stairs had been a place for friends to sit contemplating the ocean. Now they were warped into undulating curves and propped up by cinder blocks. A wreck of a man lingering in a neglected house.

"I wanted to see if your boat had been taken out in the last day." She pointed to the undisturbed sand surrounding it. "It doesn't look like it." She sighed in disappointment. "And that's the only personal boat on the island not docked at the marina, as far as I can see. I've checked up and down the beach several times. There wouldn't be any point in launching a boat on the far side, with all those rocks."

Moving forward a few steps, Henry cocked his head with dawning interest. "Why do you want to know if my boat went out?" He looked at her again and squinted in recognition. "You're Mia Spinel, right?"

She nodded, still frowning at the boat.

"I remember you from a few years ago, when I sold the hotel and most of the island. You were there with your husband." His small pig clambered awkwardly on her stubby legs down the steps, following the sound of his voice, curly tail wagging. He reached down and scratched her, smiling a little at her antics. The pig's small eyes closed in twitchy delight and she flopped on her side.

"What's her name?" Mia asked.

"Pig. Just Pig." He shrugged a little. "I wasn't really planning on keeping her to start. Couldn't just let her die, poor little thing." He looked at her sprawled across his bare feet, and she saw his mouth curve under the shaggy beard." She had other plans."

"It seems like it." Mia looked at the blissful creature with curiosity. "I've never met a pet pig before. I've heard of them, but never met one in person."

"You can scratch her head if you want," Henry offered.

"No, thank you," Mia said with decision. "I'm good." She looked at the gleam in Pig's beady eyes, intelligently assessing the intruder. "I can see why you kept her."

"Yeah," Henry straightened up. "So, why do you want to know about boats?"

Everyone else on the island knew, so she might as well tell Henry too. "I saw a body on the beach yesterday morning. A dead man with a beard."

"Woah," Henry exclaimed. "No one told me that."

"Because by the time I got back with help, the man had disappeared," Mia exclaimed with exasperation.

"Wait, is that why Evie dropped by yesterday? To see if I was still breathing?" He grinned, barely visible under the beard. "And I thought she just wanted to bring me breakfast."

"I expect she was concerned about you," Mia said. "They assumed the man must have been injured, not dead, so she checked for injured men."

"Huh." Henry turned that idea around. "Makes sense. Buck asked me if I'd seen anything odd, too. You find him?"

"No injured men found on the island, beards or not."

"A prank?" Henry proposed. "There are teenagers on the island." He cocked his head to one side. "Boys do like to play tricks."

"Maybe," Mia conceded reluctantly. "He certainly looked dead to me." She shivered slightly and explained, "His head was badly hurt." She shook her head, rejecting the idea. "He was an older man. Hard to see a middle aged man going along with kids' tricks."

Henry's eyes narrowed, "If someone moved a body off an island, they'd need a boat."

She nodded agreement.

"And I'm guessing no boats left the marina during the time between you finding the body and the body disappearing?"

"None that I saw or heard. Definitely not in those few minutes between finding the body and returning with help. The same boats are docked now that were docked the day before, in the same slips."

"Huh," Henry repeated. "Well, this puzzle calls for a drink. Come on up." He gestured to a table with two chairs on the porch, overlooking the beach.

Mia followed. "Just water for me, thanks." She sat on the proffered chair.

"Not tea? It's what I usually have about now," Henry asked again with a lopsided, unexpectedly charming smile. "I'm mostly a drunk only in the afternoons, you know."

Mia smiled back warmly. "I would love some tea, thank you.

Henry bustled into his rundown house and Mia looked around. The cushions on the worn chairs were unexpectedly new and comfortable, a bright splash of red against the gray wood. She stretched out her legs and encountered Pig.

"Oh, I'm sorry, my dear, I didn't mean to kick you." The small creature snuffled against her hand and she reluctantly scratched it, feeling the bristly hair harsh against her fingers and smiling, despite herself, at what was clearly a look of porcine bliss. Pig dropped down between the two chairs, sighing in contentment.

"Pig gets people, every time," Henry said, as he came out carrying chipped mugs. "The last thing I was planning on was a pet pig. I hope hibiscus tea's okay?"

"Hibiscus tea sounds perfect." Mia sipped the tartly refreshing, ruby red drink.

"So, you think you saw a dead body no one else saw." He looked at her appraisingly. "You don't look crazy."

"You can tell crazy just by looking?" Mia asked tartly.

"'Course I can. I've been there," he looked off into the blue horizon. "After my wife died, I went nuts for a while. Came here, to the island, where we'd always spent our vacations. Where we'd just spent our honeymoon." He squinted into the distance and blinked hard. "The island belonged to my wife's family. She was the last one left." He sighed heavily. "She died so young. We had so many plans."

"I'm so sorry," Mia told him sincerely. No one should lose a future that young.

"Your husband, Leo, right?" She nodded. "He died a year or two ago? Evie mentioned it."

"Yes," Mia said simply.

"Then you know." His brown eyes were haunted. "It's not something you get over."

"No, you never do," Mia said. "We were luckier, we had more years we shared together, but it's never easy. Never expected." She looked out across the ocean, wondering what she'd be doing with Leo now, if he was still here. "There are always so many things more you planned to do."

"I guess," Henry looked down and coughed. "So, Evie searched the island?"

"She did," Mia agreed. "Looking for an injured man."

"It's not like Evie to miss anything," Henry told her, showing clear partisanship.

"No, it's not," Mia agreed. "She's very efficient." She sipped her tea.

"She's a good woman, Evie is. When I was still going on benders, she made sure I ate. Still does, because I can't cook worth a damn." He looked at her and grinned, teeth gleaming out of his wild beard. "Delivered here when I was nuts, of course, so I didn't bother the guests. She'd sit here muttering about what an idiot I was and make me eat every bite. Absolutely ruthless."

"That sounds like Evie."

"If she said there's not an injured man on the island, there's not," he firmly concluded. He glanced over at her. "So which boats went out?"

"I can't find one," Mia said. "Yours here hasn't moved in at least a week."

"Almost two. Fishing hasn't been great next to shore lately. And you say no boats left the marina?"

She nodded. "Not when the body disappeared. Maybe later in the day, but it would have been difficult to hide it in the meantime."

"So that's all of them." He waved at the beach. "Pig and I walk up and down the beach, end to end, several times a day. Gives her some exercise," he added gruffly. "Not good for her to be cooped up all day."

"That's as good as a patrol," Mia told him.

"Yeah, that drunk, Robert, was harassing one of the women. I got to thinking, it's pretty easy to beach a boat along this coast." He gestured at the Atlantic side, his hand rough, with torn nails. "Impossible on the other side, of course."

"I wouldn't want to try it," she remembered the waves crashing on the rocky reefs.

"So I check, make sure everything's okay. Don't want Evie or the other women hassled."

"So when did you go down past the dive shop beach yesterday morning?"

"That's where you saw it?" He thought. "Later that morning, about ten."

She sighed in disappointment.

"But I also walked it about three a.m. No bodies then. I walked up and down until about five a.m."

She looked quizzically at him.

He explained. "Nice moonlit night. I don't sleep much."

"That's a tight window, but not an easy one for alibis," Mia said.

"No, most people are sleeping peacefully in their beds from five to six in the morning, if they can," Henry agreed.

"I was there when the sun was coming up. The body must have been hidden somewhere until after five, maybe in the bushes or the surf shack." She frowned, "I wonder if the murderer was moving it to a new location when I found it?"

"It's not a time many people are awake. He might have tried earlier, too, when I was walking. Good time to move a body."

"Except for me showing up," Mia said, a little glum.

"Well, it gives you something to do," Henry told her.

Mia looked at him sourly, then spotted the telltale sparkle in his eyes and burst into laughter. "I guess it does."

"And me too." He grinned cockily and she could see the happy, vibrant man he had been, only a few short years ago. "I expect I'll be better at poking into bogs looking for a dead body or boats than you. You don't look like you'd like wading through mud."

"I'll feed you a steak dinner at the end of this," Mia promised and slyly added. "If you'll shave off that beard. It's ridiculous."

"Nope. I'll have you know, this beard keeps all the tourists away." He stroked the frizzy mess. "All I have to do is glare at them and they run. Keeps things quiet."

"I'm sure it does," Mia laughed heartily. "At least trim the thing."

"Someday," Henry sighed. "Evie said she'd let me into Fritters if I looked more respectable. I do miss a good steak dinner. She's holding out on me."

"I'm completely on Evie's side," Mia said with a grin. "So you'll search the swamps and I'll check out the marina. One of those boats has to have taken the body away. There would have been just enough time to move a body from the beach to a boat, if they were very quick. Then hide it until they could take it out to dump it. There must be some signs left on the boat." She shivered sharply, her face briefly losing color. "That head wound was bad."

"I'd wash the boat off pretty well if it were me. But there's always a chance. You're nosy enough to find a trace if there's one left."

Mia drank the rest of her tea at a draught and patted Pig. "I'll see you both later."

"Happy hunting," Henry called behind her, still laughing.

As he watched the small figure of Mia striding purposefully down the beach, Henry scratched Pig's head. "Interesting problem, isn't it, girl? What do we do next?"

Pig looked up at him with her dark bright eyes.

"Right, I'm going to check out the swamps and that new construction." He frowned. "You'd better stay here, girl."

Pig looked at him, imploringly.

He shook his head firmly. "I'm not pulling you out of the swamp ooze again." He put on his sandals, clapped a ragged straw hat on his head and strode out the door toward the hotel end. Pig watched him from the window until he was out of sight, then lay down, her small feet folded delicately under her body.

Henry started at a groundskeepers shed that was being constructed. He walked around the torn up foundation, noting the concrete floor had not been poured yet. He poked purposefully around the neat stacks of concrete blocks, seeing no area a body could be hidden in. The first possibility checked off, he moved on to the nature preserve, giving the main buildings a wide berth. He didn't want to run into Evie during his hunt.

When Mia got back to the main hotel, there was a group following Buck onto the dive dock like a brood of ducklings. She tagged behind, looking at the arrangements made for a group dive. Buck checked all their equipment off and adroitly passed them on to his dive team, smiling as they splashed, one by one, into the water with their big flippers splayed wide.

Buck looked up as Mia approached. "No newbies in this lot, so the others can handle it and I can catch up on the paperwork a little. You still up for diving later today?" He waited for her answer, forehead creased in concern that she'd cancel, still annoyed with him from last night's talk.

"I'm looking forward to it," she told him with a determinedly friendly smile. "I also want to go on one of those night dives, like I saw last night. Do the corals really spawn during the full moon?" she asked curiously. "I've always wanted to see that."

"It's usually a few days after a full moon," he told her, "and a little later and hotter in the year."

"I'll have to come back, then," Mia said. "That would be amazing to see."

He nodded, then realized what she had said. "Wait, you saw divers last night? No group night dives were scheduled then. I always handle those myself, since they're much more dangerous."

"That's odd. I saw underwater lights in this area on my way back from dinner. I assumed it was a night dive on the reef."

"No, none on the schedule," he flipped back through his clipboard. frowning. "Everyone has to sign in and out, no matter what they're doing."

"Do people dive on their own?"

"After an orientation dive, we let them dive without us, but it's not encouraged. And never alone. First rule of diving." He shrugged. "Some expert divers get a little bored with the newbie groups. Can't blame them. They still have to pair up and sign in and out. And sign the insurance disclaimer." He passed a hand over his short hair. "No one should be out diving without signing out."

"What about Dr. Sebastian or his student? Surely they dive alone."

"They do, at least as a pair, but never at night. They can't count fish or corals at night, so no point." He tapped the clipboard. "And they have to sign in or out, same as everyone else. That way we know if we need to look for people and where to start looking. It's basic safety. No exceptions, not even me."

"Odd," Mia mused. "I suppose someone just forgot to sign in."

"Could you tell how many divers there were?"

"No, I only saw the lights underwater. It could have been one or twenty. Or glow sticks moving in the tide," she added with a wry smile. "It just made me want to do a night dive during my stay."

"We can do that," Buck said, still frowning at the clipboard, then glanced at the tide table, finally looking up at her with a quick grin. "I'll see you at five o'clock, if that sounds alright? The tide is perfect then."

"Wonderful. See you then." She left Buck, frowning down at his clipboard, clearly wondering how to stop dangerous illicit diving on his reef.

She sat in the same place for lunch today, ordering a crisp green salad topped with conch ceviche. She still hadn't had her fill of conch, since this island was one of the few places she ordered it.

"Delicious, Elizabeth," she told the waitress after she took a bite.

Elizabeth smiled cheerfully at her and topped off her chilled Pinot Grigio. "Wait until you see dessert," she said, clearly tempting her.

"I can't wait," Mia said with anticipation. She took a spoonful of the jicama slaw, its crunchy sweetness balanced with tart lime juice. "I've been walking on the beach this morning. Talked with Henry for a while. He seems like a nice man. Such a tragedy for him to have lost his wife so young. A shame such a nice man chose to hide away from the world."

Elizabeth nodded in agreement, "He looks a little rough on the surface, but he's a good man." She grinned slyly and winked. "He's been dropping by when Evie's leaving for the day and walking her home, lately."

"Is he now?" Mia asked with curiosity. "And does she visit there often?" she asked, remembering the bright new cushions on the porch.

"I think she drops by pretty often, but most people visit Henry when they're passing," Elizabeth confirmed. "I do like that sweet Pig."

After Elizabeth left, Mia noticed Carol sitting alone, bereft of her usual raucous crowd of young men. Carol's brow looked anxious, with her eyes hidden behind large designer sunglasses, but deeper grooves ran beside her tight mouth than had been there yesterday. She looked worried.

Thinking Carol looked like she needed cheering up, Mia went over to her table and asked, "Carol, would you like to join me for lunch?" She added, further identifying herself, "We had a yoga class together yesterday. I'm Mia Spinel," she added with a deprecating smile.

Carol looked a little startled at being approached. She had clearly been lost deep in uncomfortable thoughts. "Mia Spinel? Then it's your family who owns the hotel?"

"That's right." Mia smiled reassuringly. "My kids send me away so I don't try to set them up on any more blind dates." She grinned rakishly. "Like I'd ever dream of doing such a thing."

Carol barked a laugh and rose to her feet. She was wearing a baby blue athletic shirt and navy shorts today. "As long as you promise not to set me up either, I'd love to have lunch."

"No promises," Mia added with a mischievous smile, then laughed. "It's a deal—if you don't try to set me up either."

Elizabeth appeared from nowhere to shift Carol's drink, and Carol sat down, looking out at the ocean again. "I thought I would see Skip and his crowd by now," she frowned, tight creases appearing between her glossy sunglass lenses. "But he seems to have slept in."

"You aren't staying at his cottage?" Mia knew Skip Wilson had taken the biggest cottage on the island, so there should be plenty of room for all his group to stay there.

"No," Carol took off her sunglasses and rubbed between reddened puffy eyes, quickly veiling them again. "He and the gang are a bit too noisy for my taste." She crossed her legs and put her elbows on the table.

Mia nodded understandingly.

"And having his mom around puts a bit of a damper on his activities," her mouth twisted wryly.

"Oh, I didn't realize Skip Wilson was your son," Mia looked up in surprise.

"Not many people do. He kept his dad's name, and I changed mine back after my divorce." She shrugged, strong shoulders moving under the soft blue shirt.

"Oh, I see. That's wonderful you're here on vacation with him, but I don't blame you for wanting your space. Grown boys are a lot to handle."

"I'm really here to keep him out of trouble," Carol's brow creased again. "He got so lucky, so early in life, with his Blare app. People love it." She looked out at the marina, busy with boats. "It's a lot of pressure on him."

"It must be."

"I look after him, pull him back from doing too much. Always a mom, I guess." Carol twisted her glass, then ran a finger through the beads of condensation.

"I don't think we ever stop being moms, no matter how old kids get." Mia certainly insisted on knowing what her kids were up to, even now.

Carol continued, shrugging, "I was the CFO at my previous job, so it made sense for him to hire me for the same job at his company. Have someone he can trust." She turned her water glass slowly, making circles on the tablecloth. "Longer hours for me, but better pay. And I can keep him out of trouble. Sometimes, at least." Her shoulders drooped a little under the constant weight. "Keep him reined in a bit." Her lips tightened into a line.

"It sounds like he needs someone he can trust. He's lucky to have his mother watching over his finances."

"Yes, lots of companies fail when their financials screw up because of one crooked or incompetent employee." Carol screwed up her face, remembering, "I was with one company where the CFO ran off with most of the accounts during the holidays. Not a great Christmas for the employees. Never caught him either." She looked out at the ocean, then back at Mia. "At least I can keep that from happening to Skip."

"It sounds like you need a vacation without your son, not with him. It must be tiring, always watching over him and his business."

Carol smiled a little and ran her fingers through her short, no nonsense hair. "Yes, he's been in party mode for a year or two, so I generally skip joint vacations, except for Christmas, where I insist he behave nicely." She shook her head, "I don't need to see Skip drinking way too much and hanging out with the wrong crowd, all the wannabe Blare stars." She sighed, "He's too old to nag and not going to change until he decides to himself. All my disapproval accomplishes is me stressed and him annoyed."

She sighed again in exasperation, then suddenly laughed. "Did you know his helicopter pilot did pilot training so they could ski jump from the helicopter? Jeb had a broken leg," she rolled her eyes at Mia, "from skiing, so he was the one to do pilot training, naturally. Because he can't ski until his leg's completely healed. I swear the kid's hands shake from terror when he takes the controls. It's terrifying to ride with him."

Mia laughed. "That sounds like boy logic, if I ever heard it."

"I know," Carol took a bite of her conch chowder. "Just ridiculous. At least most of the usual suspects aren't on this trip. There're about ten more of the gang that egg each other on to do stupid stuff. Then they post it on Blare and everyone copies them, trying to best the stupidity."

"Why didn't the rest of the group come on this vacation too?" Mia asked. "Why subject you to it when it's not your thing?"

Carol frowned, narrow furrows deepening. "I don't know. Skip's worried about something. I don't know what. He only wanted his two closest friends with him, which is very unlike him, not to want the whole posse. He asked me to come this time, so of course I did." Her thin lips closed tightly and the lines on either side of her mouth deepened.

"It's nice you can be here with him, then. I'm sure it means a lot to him, to have his mom here." Mia tactfully closed the subject. "Have you been on the jungle trail yet? I'm thinking of going today."

"No, I was planning on going this morning, but I ended up just watching the waves."

"I think there's a nature walk at two o'clock, if you'd like to join me? I always like the guide pointing out the wildlife on my first visit in a while. They have such interesting stories about the animals and know exactly where the best spotting sites are. There's always something new to see."

"That sounds like fun," Carol's face relaxed a little. "You never know what you might see on a nature walk. I think I'll go too."

Elizabeth placed two plates with towering slices of key lime pie before them with a flourish. "I remembered this was one of your favorites, Ms. Mia."

"It is, Elizabeth. Thank you!" She savored a bite of the tart sweetness. "Delicious," she proclaimed.

"I probably shouldn't eat this," Carol said, tasting hers warily. "But it's so good." She took another cautious bite, clearly dreading the added calories..

"Eat it and enjoy. You're on vacation," Mia urged, taking a scrumptious bite.

"Very true," Carol smiled and deliberately carved out another forkful. "And we're going hiking later," she assuaged her conscious.

"Absolutely." Life was too short to worry about calories, Mia thought.

After lunch, Mia quickly changed into more practical clothes for a hike in the woods, a long sleeve, rose pink shirt, almost the twin of Carol's and tennis shoes to match. She headed back to the main hotel to meet the tour group, poking her head into Evie's office on the way. While still a little annoyed with Evie for enabling Buck, she did understand Evie's position and wanted to smooth things over. While making it clear she wouldn't stand for any more nonsense.

Evie looked up from her laptop, "Hi, Mia. How are you?" She regarded Mia with a wary smile.

"I'm doing well. And you?"

"Fine, everything's fine." Evie fiddled with her gold hoop earring. "Where are you off to this afternoon?" she asked, noticing Mia's unusually practical clothes.

"A nature walk, then diving the reef with Buck." Mia smiled. "I'll probably do absolutely nothing for dinner tonight."

"Absolutely," Evie agreed. "Last time I went diving with Buck, I thought I'd swum a marathon." Her round cheeks smiled at the memory and she smoothed her crown of braids. "I swear, I climbed up that ladder with my very last ounce of strength. I seriously considered just letting the tide wash me ashore. I knew I'd get back eventually." She laughed, "Never again."

Mia smiled at the idea of Evie's stately, but definitely rounded figure struggling up the ladder. "Was it worth it?"

"Absolutely," her brown eyes shone at the memory. "This one sea turtle that kept nudging me. And such bright fish all around me, like little dancing flowers." Smiling, she demurred, "When I've forgotten about that climb, I'll go back to see that cute turtle."

Sandra, dressed in her neat turquoise polo shirt and white skirt, accented today by a dramatic lime green headscarf, was gathering up stray nature explorers. "Hi, Ms. Mia, you're signed up for the walk, eh?"

"I am." She smiled at the nature group, spread in carefully spaced clumps. Going to stand next to Carol, she suddenly became concerned. Carol's face was tight and drawn, with no trace of their relaxing lunch remaining. "You look a little upset, Carol. Is something wrong?"

"I looked in at Skip's, just to check on him and to invite him to come. He's got that little tramp, Megan what's her name, over there and it's pretty obvious she'd been there all night." Her nose pinched tight. "Just after his money and a decade older than him, if she's a day."

"Oh dear."

"I know I shouldn't care who he dates, but it's hard to stop worrying about him."

"It's difficult to let our kids make their own mistakes."

"I just wish he'd have better taste in women." Carol pursed up her mouth like she'd sucked a lemon. "She's obviously out for what she can get."

"Megan doesn't seem like the most stable choice," Mia agreed tactfully. "He's still young. He'll grow out of it. So will she, I hope."

"He's not as young as he acts," Carol said through gritted teeth. She waved her arm as if to wash the memory away. "Skip was staring at his computer and barely grunted to me. That woman calls out, 'Hey mom,' and laughs like it's the funniest joke." Her nose pinched again. "She laughs like a hyena."

"She was probably drinking," Mia said tartly.

Carol sighed heavily. "She probably was." She shook her head and ran her fingers through her short hair. "I need to stop getting upset about this sort of thing. It's why I don't do joint vacations."

"Just put it out of your mind and enjoy the island," Mia advised. "If your son wants to see you, he can come find you."

Carol nodded, clearly trying to shake it off. "You're right. If he needs something, he can tell me. Otherwise, I'll enjoy my week's vacation and head on home." Her shoulders relaxed a little. "Not on that damn helicopter, either."

"That's a plan," Mia cheerfully added.

The little group fell into file behind Julie, who with the help of long khaki pants and a bright purple backpack, had transformed from yoga teacher into nature guide. Julie enthusiastically waved to Mia, "Hi, Ms. Mia! Glad you're off to explore with us!"

Looking around the group, Mia greeted Donna with a wave. She wore matching cargo pants side by side with her husband, Todd. He had a pocket filled vest and a serious looking camera, weighed down by a white lens almost as long as his arm. Amy was there for the walk, dressed in yoga pants and a sleeveless top, hair scraped back into a ponytail as usual. Mia wondered why she hadn't visited the salon while at the spa. Why couldn't people groom themselves appropriately? Of course, Amy might be planning on enjoying the salon next, after the nature trail. She'd be taking a long shower afterwards, herself.

Amy's mouth twisted sourly in obvious disappointment as she surveyed the group. Mia wondered if her husband had failed to show up for their couple's activity. Something was definitely not right in that marriage.

However, two honeymooners, with eyes only for each other, were a joy to Mia's heart. The lovebirds solicitously sprayed one another down with bug repellent. The chemical smell of heavy mosquito spray filled the air as everyone spritzed the preventative proffered by the guide. Mia was looking forward to that shower, already.

"Load up, everyone. We get to ride partway," Julie called. Everyone climbed aboard a roaring truck outfitted with hard bench seats, aided by a gap toothed young man and foldable steps. He hopped down, closed the gate with a hard thunk and they were off. Julie spoke into a little microphone and "Everyone hear me okay?" crackled out of tinny truck speakers.

"We're lucky enough to have several types of ecosystems on our one little island here," Julie crackled over the truck engine, bouncing as she held on with one hand. "The Bahamas are amazingly diverse, with so many isolated islands and cays, each containing its own ecology. A bit of elevation change is all it takes to have an entirely new ecosystem."

She pointed toward the ocean, balancing easily while the truck bounced over ruts. "We have sandy seashore on the more protected side of the island, rocky seashore on the other, which makes for completely separate flora and fauna. At the southern edge of the beach, we're fortunate in having mangrove forest, which as everyone knows, creates island where there was once only salt water. It's amazing to see how fast the island can grow. The mangroves and shore are best explored by one of our kayak tours—or just walking along the beach!"

She grinned, her short curly hair lifted up in the wind. "Today we're going to the coppices, with whiteland coppice located at the edge of the ocean. As the elevation rises and fresh water becomes available, we'll see blackland coppice, which is more what you'd think of as jungle." She shrugged deprecatingly. "We don't really have jungle in the Bahamas, just coppices." Her grin widened. "You might think you're in a jungle, until you see the real ones on the mainland!"

Mia held onto the hard wooden bench, gritting her teeth at the bumps in the rutted road and hoping she didn't get splinters in awkward areas. The truck vibrated as it steadily climbed toward the nature preserve region of the island, engine roaring loudly. At the edge of the preserve, it ground to an abrupt halt, brakes squealing, and Julie hopped out. The same cheerful man handed them down carefully, as if they were precious parcels.

They trailed Julie up the hill, ancient limestone seafloor beneath their feet. The ground was soft and powdery, easily taking precise molds of their padding footprints as they plodded up the sandy trail. Small, hardy trees dominated this landscape, acacia trees, with their long tan seedpods dangling, cacti with their wicked sharp thorns. Clearly, to survive in the whiteland coppice, plants had to be tough and spiky.

Julie paused beside one bush. "This one is Haulback. Touch it and you'll know why," she pointed at the long curved thorns waiting to pounce on visitors like a cat's claws. She mimed a clawing motion with a laugh. Everyone gave the bush a wide berth.

As they passed a large, round leafed shrub, Julie picked a few black fruits, stowing them neatly in her backpack. "Coco plums," she told them, her curls dancing in the brisk breeze. "I'm saving them for a surprise later!"

All of the group were in reasonably good shape. Mia knew Sandra would have suggested alternated activities if a guest seemed too frail for the adventure. Amy charged up the uphill path, sturdy legs moving at a constant pace, as if she was climbing a treadmill at a gym. Todd made slow progress, because of his frequent pauses to photograph a stunning vista or perching bird. Donna walked slowly and steadily, making time to enjoy her surroundings. The honeymooners clasped hands and cooed to each other, deliberately lagging behind the group.

Mia matched Carol's methodical stride, but she fell behind as she paused to take in the landscape—and to catch her breath. As they rounded each turn, sweeping vistas of the island came into view, sapphire blue sea and sky broken by the tough plants and inhospitable ground of the whiteland coppice.

The trail moved on and up, ground changing from harsh sand to soft loamy dirt as they climbed, covering the limestone like chocolate frosting on a cake. The trees gradually became taller, arching far overhead in a grand cathedral. Undergrowth turned lush and shiny green. Birds chirped and small creatures scurried under piles of leaf litter. When they could no longer see the sky above, Julie stopped. "This is our island's little stand of blackland coppice, one of the most diverse ecosystems in the world."

Streams of light filtered through the tall canopy, barely making it into the darkness of the forest floor. Massive giants of mahogany and cedar trees stood, each in their own space, with plants clinging to them as if to a ship in the ocean. Gigantic ferns stood peacock proud in the still air, with not even a breath of wind to move them.

"The original trees on the island were cut or blown down a long time ago," Julie told them. "Luckily, for a century, this island was owned by one family who had no interest in logging, so these trees have grown and thrived. It's a truly unique place."

A tiny hummingbird zoomed past the group, flaunting his bright purple throat like an amethyst necklace and making high pitched chirps. "The Bahama Woodstar," Julie said, laughing. "I think he'd like us to move on a bit."

The group laughed in response and walked up the path a few yards. "Males always do love to show off," Amy added, her face twisting in a grimace. Her legs pumped along steadily, not bothering to slow to appreciate the coppice.

Mia snarkily wondered how long before Amy's divorce was announced. Her husband obviously hadn't shown up for the nature trail, or any other of the couples occasions. She hadn't seen them communicating much at all, even during what should have been a lovely romantic dinner. The two people really didn't seem like a couple. If anything, Mia guessed Amy didn't think very much of men in general. She wondered how someone who clearly hated men had gotten married.

Mia mused that perhaps the dead man had been Amy's lover, secretly meeting her on the island, killed by her husband. Amy might not even know about his death yet, if that was true. But Amy didn't seem like she would have a lover. There was a glow about people in love, even in the secrecy of clandestine relationships, that just couldn't be faked. Amy certainly didn't have that special glow—but she might still know the dead man under other circumstances.

Mia shifted her position in the group slightly to walk next to Amy. "Look at that," she exclaimed conversationally. A massive bromeliad, with deep red leaves at its central core, hung off a mahogany tree. "Just stunning."

Amy looked, her eyes dull and uninterested. "Yeah. Pretty."

"Oh, and that orchid there." Tiny lime green and deep purple flowers hung down over the path, spiraling around a long stem.

"I like orchids," Amy seemed a bit more interested in that one.

"I read there were several species of vanilla orchids here. I've always wondered whether their flowers smell like vanilla extract."

"Maybe we'll spot one," Amy asked, interest weakly emerging. She peered into the trees.

Julie laughed gaily and pointed high up in the canopy. "See that vine growing up the tree. That's vanilla." They all followed her hand to the fleshy, pale green vine clinging to the tree, a few delicate white flowers dangling from its segmented lobes.

"I don't think we'll be able to smell it from here," Carol said dryly.

"We clearly need a lower one," Amy agreed, looking around. "But it is interesting to see it growing in the wild."

"Mmm," Donna said. "Such dainty little flowers compared to their pods. I would have thought they'd be a lot bigger, from baking with them."

"The pods go through a long curing process," Julie said. "It's not something we do here, of course," she waved high in the humid air. "Way too wet. But where they produce vanilla, they dry them in the sun for weeks. Take them inside at night, and drying in the sun every day."

"Really?" Amy asked with curiosity.

"Who would have thought such a little thing would be that much trouble to produce?" Donna mused. "But I can't imagine a kitchen without it."

"I can't either," Mia said. "Do you bake a lot?"

"I do," Donna said with a smile. "There's nothing that keeps grandkids happy like fresh cookies."

"Perfect for bribes, too."

"I know, they'll clean their rooms almost instantly when they smell cookies in the oven." Donna patted her slight tummy. "Of course, I have to make sure the kids eat most of them before I do. Way too dangerous to have in the house."

Mia chuckled. "I don't think you have anything to worry about. Did you enjoy your dive yesterday?"

"Absolutely loved it," Donna enthused. "It's like a whole other world beneath the ocean."

"It is." Mia looked forward to her dive later today.

"And this, coppice, did she say?" Donna stumbled a little on the path, looking up into the tree canopy. "This coppice is beautiful, with the deep shadows and huge, almost primeval trees. Makes me think of dinosaurs hiding in those huge ferns, long ago. The orchids are beautiful, so ethereal, but I really notice the bromeliads. Such bright colors." She sighed, "I always wanted to travel more, but between the kids and Todd's job—and now the grandkids—it just wasn't possible."

"But if he's retired now, surely you can get away some?"

"You'd think so, but he started a little consulting —he worked in cryptocurrency from the beginning, so whenever there's a problem, someone calls him in to consult." She sighed a little and her mouth drooped downwards. "He's always having to run up to New York when we have plans. Or last minute trips to Dubai or London. It's frustrating never being able to make plans for anything. He even missed my birthday last year." She added, fairly, "At least he did get me a nice present."

"At least on this last minute trip, you got to come."

"Very true," Donna agreed, then laughed. "And I'm having a great time, so why worry?" She glanced back at Todd, photographing a delicate orchid, far behind the group, and laughed, a motherly smile broad on her face. "He's having fun too. I thought he'd never get out of his meeting this morning."

The air in the coppice was heavy, closing in like a velvety blanket. Moving out of the forest, the boardwalk ended them on a short walk to the highest point in the island, craggy white limestone overlooking the entire island. Blue sea surrounded the rich greens of the little island paradise. They could see the hotel roofs far in the distance, little splashes of shingled roofs on the carpet of green, like towels on a beach.

As they reentered the darkness of the tall trees, the heavy air suddenly merged into large drops of water, hitting hard on the canopy above and trickling down to the visitors below.

Todd exclaimed and immediately shoved his camera protectively into his backpack, firmly strapping a waterproof cover over the top, then belatedly remembering to pull out a raincoat for himself and his wife from a side pocket.

Julie laughing, turned her face up to the rain. "This time of year, there's usually a shower or two." She thoughtfully pulled a stack of folded plastic ponchos out of her backpack. "Anyone need one?"

Carol laughed and said she needed a shower after the walk anyway, but Mia promptly covered herself in the clear plastic poncho.

They spotted quite a few vanilla orchids on the return loop, but never one low enough to sniff for fragrance, to Mia's intense disappointment. As they left the deep undergrowth, Mia glimpsed a satinleaf tree shimmering in a golden shaft of sun. A Bahama Yellowthroat flew into the tree, the bright yellow of its throat merging into the golden light.

As they filed out of the truck, Julie herded them into the hotel bar, smiling as she pulled the coco plums out of her backpack and placing them on the counter. "Henri, can you do something with these? These people have had a long walk and need some refreshment."

He grinned at her, "Most definitely I can." He expertly sliced and prepared the fruits, removing the hard pit from the cottony flesh, added coconut water and mint, shaking it with ice. He passed the tall frosty glasses to the group. "A nice cool drink for some thirsty walkers. You've earned it."

Mia sipped, curious at what the coco plum tasted like. The sweetness of the fruit was perfectly balanced by the mild coconut water and revitalizing tang of mint. She smiled benevolently at her walking group, then looked out on the blue ocean in pleasure.

Evie glared out her window at the beautiful view, for once taking little pleasure in the sweeping ocean vista. She inwardly sighed as she saw Mia poking in one of the boats at the marina. She was still looking for that ridiculous mythical body. Surely, she wasn't going to actually get into the boat, Evie thought. But she did. Evie watched in horror as Mia slid the boat cover aside and ducked under the canvas. Mia's shiny blonde hair bobbed in and out of view, as she obviously tried to be discreet, partially hidden under the twitching boat cover. From the passersby's stares at the woman crawling on the boat bottom, she wasn't succeeding. Evie let out an oomph of exasperation, sending her bright flowers dancing in their vase.

Why wouldn't Mia stop looking for this mythical man? Evie had checked, exhaustively. He simply didn't exist.

Much as she hated to think of Mia getting older, Evie inclined to Buck's point of view. Mia must be overtired and had imagined a body on the beach, like the murder cases she'd recently been involved in. Evie hoped it wasn't the first signs of senility in her old friend. Surely she was just under a great deal of stress right now. Evie had heard stories about the Arizona property that would give her nightmares if they happened at her hotel.

Mia didn't seem to be forgetting anything else. She certainly hadn't forgotten that damn imaginary body. But it wasn't as if she'd seen more of them or anything else.

It had been a very tiring week, even without Mia's antics. She wanted nothing more than to put up her feet and shut out the world for a day. Not much chance of that, with a demanding VIP staying and Mia acting so strangely.

Evie watched sourly as Mia clambered out of that guest's boat and into one of the hotel rentals. Surely she wasn't looking for bloodstains? Every woman knew blood was one of the easiest stains to get rid of. The rain shower earlier would have washed any trace of it away. Evie shook her head as Mia poked her head into one of the boat lockers, carefully shutting it so she didn't mar her shiny manicured fingernails. She was determined, that was certain.

Sandra stuck her head in Evie's office and Evie thankfully turned away from Mia's search antics. "We're out of that beluga caviar Skip Wilson keeps ordering. Should I send someone to Nassau to pick more up?"

"Is he eating the stuff with a spoon?"

"Probably," Sandra said, her nose wrinkled with disgust. "I'd guess with chips and salsa, from the rest of the room service menu."

Evie shuddered. "Unbelievable." Her eyes drew back to Mia, now squatting on the dock, peering into a small dinghy. "Make sure our supplier has it in stock before you send someone all the way there. Not too much call for it this season, on the islands." She shook her head. "We take care of our guests how they want, even if they're a bit crazy." She stared at Mia, now actually inside that dinghy, lifting a tarp to check underneath and squirming under it.

Sitting down with an abrupt thump, Evie rubbed her temples and loosened one of her hairpins, resettling her heavy crown of braids. "I can't wait until Skip Wilson leaves the island, but we need to take care of him to our best standards while he's here."

"Right, I'll call first, then send someone." Sandra paused a beat, her lime green headscarf cocked to one side. "You look tired. Need some coffee?"

Evie brightened a little. "Yes, please." She felt her temples throb and loosened another hairpin from her tight crown.

Sandra quietly closed the door.

Mia scrambled out of a center cockpit and sat on the edge of the dock, feet dangling. She hadn't found a thing in the boats. A few of the smaller center console boats lacked locks of any kind, leaving them open to casual thieves. No sign of any blood—or anything unusual at all.

Blood could easily be washed away, so not finding any wasn't proof the body hadn't been transported out to sea. It just meant she still didn't know where the body was.

She watched the group of divers striding down the dive dock with narrowed eyes. Any one of the guests could have stolen a boat and dumped a body. Anyone at all. She threw a leaf into the water, watching it float away on the tide.

"What are you doing with our boat?" A voice interrupted her thoughts. She looked up to see Dr. Sebastian Barbeau glaring at her.

"Is this your boat?" she asked demurely, swinging her legs around and smoothly rising to her feet. Hah, she thought to herself. That's what yoga does for you.

"I want to know what you're doing with it?" he accused again. "I saw you on it."

She held her hand out and he stared angrily at it, not moving his own. "Let me introduce myself. I'm Mia Spinel."

He rapidly backpedaled from accusation mode. "Dr. Sebastian Barbeau. Nice to meet you."

"It's nice to meet you, Sebastian," Mia said, giving no explanation about her checking out their boat. There was no believable explanation to give. "I'm so looking forward to hearing about your work on the reef. It's one of my favorite projects, you know."

"Oh, um, yeah." He looked down at his feet, clad in worn sandals. "Yeah, it's been a good place to research."

"Maybe you can show me some of your work now. I have a few minutes."

"Oh, um, sure." He gathered himself. "Sure. I work in my cottage."

"Of course," Mia agreed. "Let's go." As they took a few steps, "So tell me about what you've been doing."

He cleared his throat, smoothing his thinning brown hair. "Well, we've been counting the fish."

"Yes?"

"There's a lot of them."

"So I would expect," Mia said with asperity.

"And there's corals too, you know."

Mia cut this catalog short, "I understand you're surveying the marine life on the reef." She walked a pace. "I believe you did the original marine life survey several years ago right after the artificial reef was put into place?"

"Yes." He belatedly realized more was called for. "I did, surveyed it before and immediately after. There was practically nothing here a few years ago, some fish, but no corals."

"And now there are more fish?" Mia prompted.

"And corals," he quickly added, increasing his stride.

"What types of fish and corals?" This conversation was like slogging through sand.

He quickly cut in, "And other marine life, of course. Panulirus argus, Aliger gigas, Echinoderms, Cheloniidae, all sorts of marine life has appeared."

Mia latched on to the last scientific name with relief. "I do love sea turtles. What kinds have you seen?"

"Chelonia mydas and Eretmochelys imbricata, mostly. I did spot one Dermochelys coriacea at a distance, but naturally it swam out of sight before I could examine it further."

"How nice." Mia decided to do a little review of the scientific nomenclature in her guidebook before her next conversation with Dr. Barbeau. She was pretty sure Chelonia mydas was a green sea turtle, but she was admittedly lost on the rest.

The research fellowship cottage was set inland from the guest cottages, with a view of palm trees and undergrowth, not white sand beaches. There was a large living room, desks lining one wall and two bedrooms, plenty of room for a researcher and one or two interns. The hotel had planned for everything a researcher might need for a few months on the island.

He entered the cottage, leaving her to follow. Mia stepped inside and immediately wished she hadn't. The place wasn't at frat house stage, probably because the housekeepers visited regularly. However, paper was everywhere. Stacks of notebooks piled on the counters, charts taped to the walls, a blizzard of post-it notes and printed graphs and databases everywhere, like scientific confetti. It was an absolute mess.

"How can you find anything in this?" Mia asked, aghast. Her feet slipped on a book lurking beneath a stack of paper. There was no path into the room, just piles of paper and books, with vibrant candy wrappers adding occasional pops of color. The floor was sticky.

He shoved some reference books off the couch and motioned for her to sit on the little cleared island. The only other usable chair was at his desk. He pivoted into his place, the well of piled paper preventing the rolling chair from any movement whatsoever. "Oh, I can lay my hand on everything fairly quickly." His monitor screen was so covered in post-it notes she could barely see the light of the screen.

Mia shifted her feet. Paper crackled underneath. "But if you had some sort of filing system..."

He looked at her, clearly not understanding. "I think of the whole room as my file cabinet, really. That way I know where everything is."

Mia said nothing. It was really the nicest thing she could say.

He swung to his computer, printing out more murdered trees. The pages organized themselves directly onto the floor, spilling off to join their brethren. He scooped up some of the lost ones and handed them to her. "Here's our latest data by the month. We're really seeing a lot of activity around the reef as it warms up."

Mia took his database with trepidation. It was surprisingly organized. She quickly shuffled the papers into order and stacked them neatly. "Thanks, Sebastian. I'll take a look at this, then perhaps we can have dinner tonight?"

"Yeah, yeah. Dinner tonight." He scribbled a post-it note and added it to his monitor flock.

Mia made a mental note to send someone to remind him about his dinner plans. "Is there anything in particular that I should look for in this?"

"I dunno." His fingers grated against his two day stubble. "I think the corals are getting interesting. I was surprised at how quickly the Scleractinia colonized the reef, especially Acropora muricata."

Mia wasn't going to be stumped on that one. Alec, Mia's stepson, had once enthusiastically kept a saltwater aquarium. "Staghorn corals are some of the fastest growing corals, so it's not surprising they've colonized it first."

"True," Sebastian said avidly, scrawny arms spread wide. "It's a good sign, however."

"A very good sign," Mia agreed. She stood up, paper shifting under her feet, propelling her toward the door. "I look forward to dining with you, then. Please do tell your intern to come as well."

"I'll see you then." He swung back around to his desk, not bothering to see her out.

Under Water

Mia tugged on her tight fins, then padded awkwardly over to the edge of the dock. Clambering down, she felt the wood shake as Buck dropped to sit beside her, lifting the heavy tanks onto her back and checking the fit. The tank dragged her down and she was grateful to be sitting.

At last satisfied, he patted her on the shoulder. "You look good to go. Any adjustments you need?"

She shook her head, putting her regulator into place, tasting the rubbery plastic with a grimace. She gave a quick, hard shove off the dock and splashed in the water, the heavy weight of the tank easing immediately as she sank down. She breathed in slowly and regularly, allowing her body to easily adjust to the first ten feet. White rippled sand stretched out beneath, broken only by the occasional bright flash of a fish. Keeping her eyes on Buck's dark fins slowly kicking ahead of her, she allowed him to guide her to the budding reef.

With increasing depth, the sandy bottom became tinged blue and dotted with an occasional sea fan, delicate fronds gently waving in the current, or the silvery gleam of a barracuda. Sunlight streamed through the water, leaving oscillating patterns on the sand below.

Buck kicked out smoothly, swimming deeper. Swallowing hard as she felt her ears adjust to the greater depth, she followed. A parrotfish with purple pink lips swam past her arms, its bright blue body leading her downward.

The limestone boulders that had formed the original reef began to appear in the smooth sand, creating small safe havens where darting schools of fish clustered, taking refuge before daring the open water between. Long ago scraped clean and scattered by dredging, corals were once again taking root in tiny crevices in the rock they had built. The bright purple of a sea fan swayed in the current, circled twice by the parrotfish, watching to see where these interlopers were going.

Buck swam slowly deeper, allowing for gradual acclimation, and Mia followed, the curious parrotfish trailing behind.

Concrete structures, like a giant's game of jacks, came into view in the blue tinged water. The arms of the jacks interwove, creating a strong barrier protecting the sandy hotel beach from being washed away in a Caribbean storm. Small corals had already started colonization of the rough concrete, with their multitude of holes making perfect hiding places for small creatures. A cluster of bright red and white Christmas tree worms anchored to one jack arm, making a cheerful decoration. As Mia passed close, her shadow made them furl into tight little cocoons. Pausing a minute to watch, she saw them unfurl into beautiful miniature trees, gently swaying. The next concrete arm held even more, and she carefully watched them, red and white in multiple spiraling patterns, punctuated by intense blue and sunshine yellow. Their arms pulsed in the current, waiting for their food to come to them.

The golden yellow head of a jawfish popped out of its burrow, its four inch long body bright blue against the pale sand. Its giant eyes watched Mia to see if she was a threat. Evidently not, as more yellow heads popped up, gazing around to see the latest news.

Spiny sea urchins tumbled along the reef jacks, grazing for vegetation to munch on. At these sunlit shallow depths, these roving urchins kept the nascent corals free from algae, preventing them from being smothered by a thick green blanket.

Up ahead lay the sunken barge forming the cornerstone of the artificial reef. The barge had been cleaned and stripped before being sunk to the bottom of the sea. The hundred feet of its bulk was already well colonized, in part thanks to the seeding of tiny coral fragments the reef building team had anchored all over the ship. Each fragment was tied on or wedged into the reef, giving it a chance to take hold and grow.

The reef building was going better than expected, since just down the beach lived a few fragile fragments of an ancient, still intact reef. Native species didn't have far to go to find their new home. They just needed the chance to grow. Hence the biodiversity was much greater than most human built reefs could create in this amount of time, no matter how many tiny corals you stuck on a new reef. Nature was much better at filling gaps than humans could ever be. They'd just given her a helping hand.

The giant jacks surrounding the reef area further protected the barge from storms by dissipating strong currents before they could destroy the fragile ecosystem. Several massive reef balls, half circles pock marked with holes for wildlife, were scattered around the outskirts of the barge. Eventually, they should help blur the edges of the sunken barge, making it a more natural appearing reef. It would be decades before that happened, but the Spinels always planned for the future. Mia knew her grandchildren would someday be able to dive this reef and appreciate new wonders.

Part of the reef blocks stretched overhead as Mia swam downward, still placed shallowly enough for snorkelers to enjoy seeing the fish below and perhaps play at a little free diving. But once you left the sun kissed shallows, there was so much more to explore.

The red of Mia's wetsuit gradually morphed to a soft pink as the sunlight filtered through deeper water. They were now about thirty-five feet below the surface. They wouldn't be diving much deeper here, but lingering at this dangerously beautiful depth in diving. There was plenty of light to see by, here in the shallow depths, but the surface seemed so temptingly close that new divers had to be reminded to ascend slowly. Immersion in this wonderful world beneath the sea was worth the risk, but it did come with dangers attached.

A beautiful angelfish, bright blue with yellow fins, swam gracefully to one of the reef balls, disappearing into a hole. Mia swam down to see where it had gone and spotted the bright shine of silver resting on the sand. Hoping for a Spanish doubloon, but even while knowing the impossibility of a shiny coin keeping its polish in the sea, she went closer to investigate. A stainless steel man's watch, newly bright and obviously not exposed to the ocean long, was only lightly blurred by sand. One of her guests must have dropped their watch, she decided, and placed it on her wrist where it hung like a heavy clunky bracelet.

Buck came up, curious what she was doing, and she pointed to the watch and shrugged. He nodded with understanding and waved to her to follow.

The low barge was long, and the forming reef made even longer by the reef balls and jacks, as well as limestone rubble. She liked the softening of the manmade lines happening already with the sea fans and cupped columns of sea sponges. The reef build had been a massive project she and Leo had always dreamed of, as well as a massive expense for the family company, so she was glad it was coming together so well. In a few decades, it would be difficult to tell where the artificial reef ended and the natural one began.

A school of bright blue angel fish swam by, leading them along the side of the barge. A starfish scuttled smoothly along the sandy bottom, blue in the filtered light. Buck pointed at a massive hole in the barge side, clearly asking her if she wanted to enter. She peered into the dark water inside, then shook her head no. Without supplemental lighting, it would be difficult to enjoy the experience. Swimming through dark holes might be fun for thrill seekers, but she preferred to see this magical world unfolding around her. Buck continued down the line of the barge, swimming around sunken reef balls.

Each little grouping of reef balls and rubble created pockets on the ocean floor, small worlds of their very own. Small fish and, she smiled at the sudden appearance of a moray eel, others made their homes in a particular crevice, perhaps never even leaving their protective shelter in their lives. A crab, no bigger than her finger, waved his large claw in fierce defense of his hole, daring her to come closer. Creatures like the school of angel fish still guiding her or the nurse shark silkily gliding from one neighborhood to the next, travelled through the reef, hunting for food.

They passed the end of the barge and Buck motioned, did she want to come back by the ocean side or return the same way? After a moment's hesitation, she pointed toward the deep ocean. She knew they wouldn't be going out to the big drop of the shelf into the depths— it needed a boat to safely take them that far. The barge had been precisely sunk on a small limestone shelf, where the ocean side was much deeper than near the island. The island side of the juvenile reef would probably be the more interesting side, since it was protected by the island itself, but she was curious what had settled around the ocean side.

At first, it didn't seem like much was living in the deeper blue water. A few sea fans, ghostly in the pale light, had settled on the wreck. A cluster of sponges clung to the side. A spiny lobster guarded the entrance to his hole under one of the sea jacks, his tentacles waving in the current. A large grouper lumbered by, making his way through the hazy water as steadily as a tanker ship. As she swam further, her eyes adjusted to the blue depths, noticing the flow of life around the deep reef.

A black tip shark swam overhead, the shadow on the sand below startling her for a moment as she stared up at its smooth prowling glide, reminding her that here, she was prey as well as predator. A group of shiny jacks swam by, gleaming like armor in the blue light.

She saw the blue angelfish school dancing on the other side of the jacks, and she went closer to see what they were doing. Their bright striping dulled in the dim light, but she laughed as they shimmered through the water, weaving in and out off reef balls and jacks like a flock of birds, pausing to nip at waving strands of algae clinging to the concrete. She swam closer, curious to know if they were damaging the reef or simply grooming them of algae.

Beyond the protective concrete jack, the deep blue of the ocean stretched out, seemingly forever. She gazed into the depths, mesmerized by its vast wonder.

Buck swam up and lightly touched Mia's shoulder, then his watch. She nodded understanding and turned to go, taking one last look. As her gaze focused, she saw a familiar shape lying on the rippled sand of the deeper ocean floor, the body of a man.

She tapped Buck and pointed fervently.

She saw him mouth what she was sure was a curse around his regulator. His hand firmly gave her an unmistakeable signal to stay where she was. He swam towards the underwater figure and circled twice, assessing the situation. She followed, staying well behind and at shallower depths.

She got close enough to tell it was the same bearded man she'd seen on the beach and very, very dead. His legs and arms were tied to concrete blocks. His body floated in the current, trying to leave the sand, but tethered by the blocks. His face was horribly distorted by his time on the sea floor. She turned away quickly, not wanting to see more of the ocean's damage.

She swam slowly back to where Buck had told her to stop and waited. He took his time examining the body, eventually swimming back to her with a grim face.

There was no dallying on the rest of the return trip. Buck set a pace Mia was hard pressed to follow him at, inextricably moving upward, acclimating as they swam homeward. The water felt thick and viscous, fighting her every move and the tank and dive gear might as well have been an anchor. Her legs pounded and burned in the buffeting water, feeling like they couldn't possibly move any faster. Then Buck upped the pace again.

Mia saw the straight wood legs of the dock with what would have been a deep sigh of relief, if she'd had enough air left in her lungs for that. She was tempted to just lie in the water and let the tide carry her to shore, but she had to get out of her heavy gear.

They climbed the ladder and stripped off their detachable gear, whereupon Mia collapsed, lying down on the smooth wood of the dock.

Buck stood over her, his figure blotting out the sun. "I owe you an apology, Mia. A big one."

She shook her head, too exhausted to care any more.

"It'll be a good one when I make it," he assured her. "Right now, I need to call the police. There's a storm heading in tonight." He helped her out of the tank, then strode briskly down the dock.

She belatedly nodded understanding, lying still on the dock for just a few more minutes until her breath returned. Then she stripped off the uncomfortable wet suit. Wrapping herself in her white linen coverup, she headed for her cottage and a long cleansing shower.

Evie looked up as Buck stepped into her office, quietly closing the door behind him. Startled by the set look of his narrowed eyes, she asked, "What's wrong?"

"We found Mia's body."

"Mia's body?" Evie asked, aghast. Her face went white as she abruptly stood up.

"No, no, Mia is fine. The body she saw on the beach." Buck shook his head as Evie slowly collapsed into her chair. "Sorry. You know, the one we called her crazy for. That body."

Evie put her hands to her crown of braids and tugged hard. Two stray braids tumbled out. "A body? At my hotel?"

"A body at your hotel," Buck repeated patiently.

Evie sat back down with a thump, her well padded body collapsing into the soft chair. "What do we do now?"

"We call the police." Buck's face was grim.

"Is that really necessary?" Evie's previous experiences with the local police had been trying, to say the least. Their meticulous search of the guest and staff rooms when drugs had been found on a recent hotel guest had been extremely disruptive. She appreciated that the police had to search, but wished they had been more discreet about doing it. Several uninvolved guests had left as a result.

"Evie, the man was tied to a concrete block and dumped in our reef," Buck said flatly.

Her eyes widened in shock. "I thought a diver had had an accident. Crawled back out to sea or something?" Her tone hoped he would change his statement.

"No accident. Murder," Buck said shortly. "You want to call or you want me to?"

"No, I'll call." Evie picked up her phone. "A concrete block? Not really?" Her soft brown eyes begged him for a different answer.

Buck just looked at her. Gritting her teeth, she reluctantly dialed the police.

As Buck went forward to greet the police boat, he felt Mia's eyes boring into his back from her perch on the balcony. It took a little effort not to turn around to glare at her, but he managed to keep his outward attention on the neat blue shirts of the police officers.

A short, trim man wearing a crisp khaki uniform held his hand out. "You must be Mr. Buck Jaeger, the man who found the body?"

"That's right."

"I am Detective Albury, in charge of finding the truth of this dreadful tragedy." His solemn face showed rigid determination. "I understand you are in charge of dive operations here at the hotel?"

"Yes."

"Then I'll question you now and have you guide the police divers to the body's location afterwards, if you don't mind." His set tone said Buck would be guiding them there, even if he did mind. And they'd be keeping a close eye on him too.

"Of course." Buck told him everything he knew.

When he had finished his story, Detective Albury looked up from his small notebook. "This guest, Mrs. Mia Spinel, she was with you when you found the body?"

"She was," Buck said guardedly. He glanced up at Mia's big pink hat and quickly averted his gaze.

"Who saw it first, you or she?"

"She did."

"And this same guest, she was the one who reported a body on the beach? A body that subsequently disappeared?"

"Yes." Buck fought the urge to shuffle his feet. He didn't like the direction this questioning was headed in.

"Why didn't you report this at the time? It's a bit unusual to have a report of a dead body and not call the police." Detective Albury's clear brown eyes held his steadily. "Surely a guest reporting a body on the beach doesn't happen every day?" he inquired with gentle sarcasm.

Buck tried to explain the blunder away. "We thought she must have made a mistake, that the man was only sick, since we couldn't find anyone of that description. Mrs. Spinel is an old friend and here for a much needed vacation. She's been overdoing it lately." He ground to a halt, realizing the multiple explanations were digging him in deeper, making him look guilty. None sounded very believable now, with that body in the water, tied to a concrete block.

"Really," the detective stated with disbelief. "An old friend? Overdoing it?" He looked at Buck sharply, "Is she mentally unstable? Frequently sees dead bodies and that sort of thing?" His gaze sharpened. "Spinel? Not related to the owners, is she?"

Buck held his hands up, "No, no." He shook his head, feeling Mia's sunglasses glaring at him. "I didn't mean to give you that impression." He shrugged helplessly, "We just couldn't find the body. There was no body." He added, "Mrs. Spinel is one of the hotel owners, yes. But there wasn't any body to be found. We looked."

Albury wrote quickly, while keeping an eye on Buck. "Still, an incident of that kind appears to be rather worth reporting to the local police, no matter the unpleasant publicity. It seems quite odd you failed to report the sighting." Detective Albury continued, "I'll need to talk with Mrs. Spinel as soon as possible." He snapped his notebook shut, neatly tucking his disposable pen into the spiral loop.

"Of course." Buck nodded up at the balcony and Mia's enormous straw hat blotting out part of the background. "She's right up there, under that big hat. I'm sure she'll tell you everything she knows."

"I'm sure she will," Detective Albury smoothly agreed, clearly not buying Buck's statement. "If that's all you can think of, I think I'm finished with you for now. If you would be so kind as to guide the recovery team..." his obvious order trailed off politely.

"Sure, let me get my suit back on and I'm ready to go. I'll meet their boat at the dive dock where my gear is stored. I can take the police boat directly to the body." He pointed over to it.

"Thank you."

Buck could feel the detective's thoughtful eyes assessing him as he walked down the long stretch of the dock.

Mia watched as the police boat moved alongside the dive dock and Buck leapt aboard, carrying his tank, before they even had time to throw him a mooring line. Billowing gray clouds on the horizon meant they'd better hurry to get the body out of the sea before the storm. From what she'd seen on the radar, there was no guarantee that body would still be there tomorrow. It had disappeared once already, after all.

She was hungry after her afternoon hike, followed by the strenuous dive. Mia took a long drink of her cool switcha, planning an early dinner after her meeting with the police. She was quite sure they would want to meet with her soon, so there was no point in making them chase her down. Always better practice to make life easier for law enforcement.

She curiously watched the boat slowly making its way out to the reef site, Buck hanging over the side and checking the GPS on his wrist computer to pinpoint the location. The boat paused with a wave of his hand, rolling slightly in the waves. Buck flipped over the side of the boat, followed by three police divers. She hoped the police wouldn't damage the reef if they anchored, then noticed Buck hand delivering the steel anchor to the bottom. Smart of him to think of that. Mia shivered, not feeling so hungry any more.

The lead detective briskly strode up the hotel stairs and entered, followed by two police officers in neat blue uniforms. Only one officer was left on board the distant boat. He alternated impatiently peering over the side to look at the divers and watching the looming clouds of the encroaching storm.

In a few minutes, Elizabeth brought the expected summons with a distressed grimace. Would Ms. Mia mind stepping into the manager's office? At her convenience, of course.

Mia entered Evie's office, noticing Evie slumped behind her desk, her braids coming loose and her usual vibrant energy depressed. The officer, attired in an immaculate khaki uniform with all creases sharply ironed, held out his hand. "Mia Spinel?"

"Yes," she acknowledged. "Evie, is there a conference room not in use where the police can set up their temporary office?" She turned to the detective. "I assume you'll need to question a lot of people, not just me." Mia wanted the police out of the main hotel building as quickly as possible. A murder investigation had to happen, of course, but she wanted it to happen away from uninvolved guests.

Evie looked up, her lassitude breaking slightly with the simple task. "There is an empty conference room at the center." She asked the officer. "Would that be useful? I can have it ready immediately."

"It's not far from here?"

"No, a few buildings down."

He nodded, considering. "That sounds ideal." He turned to Mia. "Can you direct me?"

"Of course," Mia agreed.

Evie looked thankful to get the policeman out of her office. She picked up the phone with her plump, manicured hand. "It'll be set up by the time you get there," she assured them.

Mia led the police officer out of the hotel and down the pretty grass lined sidewalk to the conference center. "This building will be a more private place to question people, I think." She smiled, a little facetiously. "And much more discreet for the hotel."

He nodded his tacit understanding, fully aware of the money and jobs the Spinel Reef Resort brought into the area. He added in clipped tones, "I'll be as discreet as possible, but my primary concern is to catch a murderer." His brown eyes looked frankly at her, secure in his primary duty.

"Of course," Mia smoothly agreed. "And the faster you catch the murderer, the less bad publicity there is for the hotel. We'll do everything possible to help you." She added, "I didn't catch your name?"

"Detective Albury," he said guardedly, clearly wondering if she was planning on contacting his superiors to rush him through his investigation.

"Well, Detective Albury, if there is anything you need from me or the Spinel Reef Resort to clear up this terrible crime quickly, please let me know."

"Thank you," he said, his eyes shifting awkwardly. "First, I want your statement on precisely what happened."

They entered the bare conference room. A gleaming mahogany table surrounded by comfortable chairs, several small tables and additional chairs lined up along the wall greeted them. A large screen and several local wildlife paintings decorated the walls. Detective Albury assessed the room, "This will work."

With the ease of long routine, a police officer accompanying him sat down and pulled out his neat notebook, placing a phone beside it to record the interview.

Detective Albury took out his own notebook and Mia settled in a linen upholstered chair, crossing her legs. "Where should I begin?"

"When did you first notice anything wrong at the hotel?" He looked at her, clearly gauging her truthfulness.

"When I found the body on the beach." She shuddered once, hard, then got herself under firm control.

"Then that's a good place to start."

He asked innumerable questions, surprising Mia with his prompts of things she had noticed at the time, but forgot to mention. She described Evie's search for an injured guest and subsequent failure to find any men fitting Mia's description. Then, she admitted her own hunt for the man, culminating in the deep sea dive.

"You've had quite a day or two, Mrs. Spinel," Detective Albury told her.

"It's been busy," she admitted, with a wry smile. "I hope you're able to discover that poor man's identity and catch his murderer soon. I don't like to think of a murderer running loose at my hotel."

"I don't like unsolved murders in my division," Detective Albury agreed. "Unfortunately, from what you said, his face won't be recognizable, even if he had been a guest at the hotel."

"No," she shuddered a little. No one could recognize his face now.

"Do you think you could work with a sketch artist to get a better idea of what he looked like?"

"No," she told him, to mutual disappointment. "I don't think I could. His face was mostly turned into the sand in my brief glance. All I can tell you is he had a short beard, dark hair—at least dark when wet—and light skin."

"And the clothes, of course. Common ones, at that." Detective Albury's brown cheeks deflated a little as he sighed. "Well, it's not much to go on, but odds are he's a visitor to our sunny shores since he turned up at a hotel beach. I'll see if there's anything in Immigration."

"That sounds promising," Mia said hopefully. "Well, detective," she began her retreat as the door slammed open hard enough to make her jump.

"Where's the police?" A wild-eyed Skip Wilson burst into the room. "I want police protection, now!" He aggressively advanced toward the police, leaning in over Detective Albury, and Mia saw the young officer quickly switch his hand from his pen to his firearm. "I demand police protection."

Detective Albury didn't even blink at the invasion. "I understand you have a problem, sir. Please take a seat." As Skip hesitated, he repeated, "Now, sir."

Skip dropped into a chair. His ratty board shorts crunched with salty sand and he'd neglected to put on a shirt, showing his sunburned, cadaverous chest. "Do you know who I am?" he accused with his mouth twisted. "If you don't protect me, I'm going to call your boss. No, your boss's boss!" he added smugly

"Yes, sir." Detective Albury calmly turned to the next page in his notebook and his pen hovered at the first line. "If you'll please give me your name?"

"I'm Skip Wilson, dammit," he snapped, tapping his foot on the floor.

The detective calmly wrote Skip Wilson on the first line, omitting the expletive. "What seems to be your concern, Mr. Wilson?"

"Someone's trying to kill me!" he rolled his eyes like a teenager explaining the latest trend.

"Really." The detective was clearly unimpressed. "And why exactly would someone try to kill you?"

Skip's flipflop smacked the floor as he stamped like a petulant two year old. "They're after me. I'm telling you, they want to kill me." His face clearly reflected conflicting thoughts. He threw out, "They, they want my money. You know."

"I see," Detective Albury replied. "Do you have a lot of money?"

"Dammit, I'm Skip Wilson." He blew out his cheeks in exasperation.

"I see," repeated the detective, who had clearly never heard of Skip Wilson, but was loathe to give up his original assumptions, based solely on the man's lack of a wardrobe. "Have you had this kind of thing happen before? Do people usually try to kill you?" he asked in soothing tones.

"It's why I'm on this miserable island, isn't it?"

"This miserable island," he murmured as he wrote it down. "You're not here on vacation?"

"Does it look like I'm here on vacation?" Skip said scathingly. His bare sunburned chest and flip flops screamed otherwise. "Here? At this hotel? Do I look like I vacation at these types of places?" His words dripped with sarcasm.

Mia bristled at the slur to her hotel, but kept her mouth firmly shut, curious to hear why Skip was actually here. She certainly didn't want people like him at her lovely resort.

"Why are you here, then?" Detective Albury inquired patiently.

"Uh, look, I'll have to get back to you on that." Skip's eyes darted around the room. "Look, your policeman said I can't leave the island. And I have to leave the island right now because someone's trying to kill me. A bunch of hick police aren't going to be able to protect me."

Detective Albury explained with exaggerated care, "You haven't clearly explained why this unknown man's murder is a threat to you, sir."

"I just told you so."

They glared at each other, locked in a stalemate like two bulls fighting. Finally, Skip's eyes dropped. "Look, I just know it, okay?"

"Please tell me a little more about your problem, sir. Then I'll be able to help you."

"Yeah, yeah," Skip capitulated. "I don't know, I'm not supposed to discuss it."

"Who told you that?"

"The government."

"What government? The Bahamian Government?"

"No, why would I listen to them? The US Government. They're supposed to have people here protecting me." He shrugged. "They sure slipped up on that one, with people getting killed."

"Why would the United States Government have someone on the island protecting you?"

"Look, I can't tell you that." Skip expelled air with irritation.

"I see," repeated the detective, narrowing his eyes. "Well, this is our initial investigation of a homicide. During this time period, no one is allowed to leave the island. There are no exceptions."

"You can't keep me prisoner here!" He stamped his foot again, flipflop abruptly slapping on the tile floor.

"I sincerely hope it won't be for long," Detective Albury assured him, obvious truth in his disgusted expression.

"I'm calling your superiors," Skip blustered. "This will cost you your job."

"Mr. Wilson, do you have anything pertinent you can tell me about this man's death?"

"No, I don't," Skip yelled at him petulantly. "I'm not telling you a thing since you won't let me leave the island."

"Then you're free to leave this room, but not the island while we're conducting our initial investigations."

"This is false imprisonment!" Skip stomped out of the conference room, slowing to a hop, as he lost one flipflop and shoved it back on.

"Am I free to go, Detective Albury?" Mia asked politely. "It's been rather a long day."

"Of course, Mrs. Spinel. I'll let you know if we have any further questions." His penetrating brown eyes glanced at Skip retreating and narrowed as they swung back to Mia. "I feel certain I'll see you later."

Mia nodded and hurried to catch up with Skip. She caught up to his uneven stride.

"Mr. Wilson?"

He snarled as he faced her. "What do you want?"

"I'm Mia Spinel, one of the resort owners."

"So?"

"I wanted to ask if there was anything the hotel could do to make you feel safer while you're waiting to leave the island." It was the only thing she could think of.

"I have a security guard."

"Yes, but one man, by himself, couldn't possibly cover your entire cottage adequately."

Skip's eyes darted nervously.

"I have an idea," Mia said. "Our head of dive operations is an ex Navy Seal. He might be able to check in to give your man a break and offer some ideas for your protection."

"Ex Navy Seal, huh?" Skip looked thoughtful and shrugged. "Sure, why not?"

"His name is Buck Jaeger. I'll send him over as soon as possible."

"Okay." Skip kept his beeline to his cottage.

Mia grinned wickedly, her eyes dancing with triumph. A few hours with Skip and Buck would know everything that kid knew. And Mia would have the start of her payback for Buck calling her crazy.

7

On the Move

Back at her cottage, Mia noticed the watch she'd found on the ocean floor. The Bulova watch hadn't been immersed long enough to tarnish the stainless steel or dim the glass, only a few days at most. She picked up the heavy watch, looking for an inscription on the back. "With all my love, Judy," her finger traced the elegant script.

Well, it was definitely a man's watch, not a woman's, so the name didn't help much. But perhaps a Judy was still staying at the hotel with her husband. If not, the name might be in a recent guest list. The watch still ticked away, undeterred by its time beneath the sea. The left side was scratched slightly, with even a mark or two etched into the crystal, so the man must be left handed, or at least wore his watch on his right hand. It had obviously been a thoughtful gift since it had been worn often.

Mia carefully placed it in her pocket for Evie to hopefully restore to the rightful owner.

Buck knocked briskly on the door of Skip Wilson's cottage. After a minute, it cautiously opened, but only to the limits of the security chain. Skip's security guard stood in full view and truculently demanded, "What do you want?"

Buck noted, with an inward sigh, that he could have shot the bloated guard and kicked in the door already. This dumb kid had no excuse for calling himself a security guard—he wouldn't even make it as an empty warehouse security guard. Still, he had to work with what he had.

"Hello, I'm Buck Jaeger, head of dive operations on the island. Mrs. Spinel asked me to drop by and help out with your security." Do something about your lack of security, was what he wanted to say, but he held his tongue.

In a flash, the door closed, the chain slid back and he was welcomed inside with relief. Buck sighed to himself again. The fool hadn't even asked him for identification. "I understand Mr. Wilson is currently in a high risk situation." With no reason for that at all, as far as Buck could tell.

The so-called security guard wore a sleeveless t-shirt showcasing bulging arm muscles that had been clearly inflated with a bicycle pump, so grotesque was the isolated muscle development. Gym shorts with a pudgy belly hanging over them—and flip flops completed the inauspicious look. Buck looked down at the flip flops and pointedly asked, "Can you run in those things?"

The kid looked like Buck had asked if he could fly, then light slowly dawned. He shuffled out to change his shoes. Buck doubted he could run even with adequate footwear.

The once elegant living room of the cottage was a mess. Discarded candy wrappers, game consoles and plates from room service mounded every horizontal surface. Buck knew housekeeping would never let it remain like this for more than twenty-four hours. It was a heck of a lot of rubbish for one day.

Skip sprawled on the sofa in the middle of it, like a bird roosting in his fouled nest. His arms lay across the back of the sofa, marking his territory, a purring Megan snuggled into his side. His bare feet were propped on the coffee table. He challenged Buck with a belligerent stare, "So, you think you can keep me safe? Or at least get me off murder island?"

Megan sat up slightly, placing a pink nailed hand on Skip's leg. In a shrill voice, she demanded, "You can't just keep us trapped here, you know."

Buck regarded Skip steadily for a long minute, letting just a hint of his disgust show. "I don't quite understand why you didn't inform security you might be in danger before you arrived?"

Skip glared back at him, tapping one hand along the back of the sofa. "I brought my own security. What business is it of theirs?"

"You have one security guard," Buck stated flatly.

Bud sidled back into the room. "I've been here the whole time."

"He wins every time at Call of Duty," Skip bragged. "Got more kills than anyone. And he pumps more iron than anyone else at the gym." Chortling, Skip added, "You won't catch me at a gym."

Everyone in the room laughed sycophantically. Megan wiggled down next to Skip's side.

Indeed, Buck thought as, with an effort, he managed not to roll his eyes. "While I'm sure, Bud, is it?" Bud nodded, and grabbed a beer. "Is an," he winced visibly at the lie, "adequate guard under normal circumstances, if you are genuinely concerned about a targeted attack, you should have a team of at least five trained guards as security staff. Minimum." He added, "Even highly trained protection has to sleep sometimes."

"That's what I said," Jeb put in. No one listened to him.

"But how do I know they're not the ones trying to kill me? Or paid assassins?" Skip whined. "If I knew who wanted me dead, I wouldn't have a problem, now, would I?" he said defiantly. "I could hire anyone."

Buck leaned casually against a wall. There were no visible seating surfaces left. "So, tell me why you think someone's trying to kill you?"

"I know someone's trying to kill me," Skip yelled. "That's why I'm at this lousy third rate hotel."

"I don't understand. You're here on the island because someone's trying to kill you?" Buck didn't even flinch at the insult to his hotel, but he boiled inside.

Skip stood up, shrugging Megan's clinging hand off, and started pacing, dodging detritus. He ran his fingers through his thinning brown hair, making it stand up straight in dandelion tufts. Moving restlessly, he finally stopped with both hands on the wall, head bowed down. "Look, I can't take this anymore, guys." He hit the wall with his fist, hard, and winced.

Shaking his hand, Skip crashed down on the sofa again, arms held protectively over his concave chest. Megan scuttled over to soothe him. He ignored her, complaining, "They sent me here. They said I'd be safe and I'm obviously not safe. It's all their fault, not mine."

"Who sent you here?"

"Those incompetent federal agents. The two they sent to meet me here." Skip tugged his hair tufts even higher.

"What federal agents?"

Skip rolled his eyes. "I'm not supposed to tell anyone I'm working with them." He fumbled in his laptop bag. "There were photos and docs, lemme see." He scrolled through his phone for an awkward amount of time. "I dunno where it went. Doesn't matter, I mean, they're here, they can tell you."

Buck guessed, "The Smiths, right?" Federal agents at his hotel, dammit. He should have spotted them sooner.

They just hadn't fit his federal agent mental profile—he must be slipping.

Skip's mouth dropped open. "How'd you know that?"

Buck shrugged. Two agents working together—not exactly a stretch they were the oddly matched couple pretending not to know Skip, while the husband spent hours at his cottage. "Who are they protecting you from?"

"I don't know," Skip yelled and threw a plate at a wall. It shattered, dripping tomato sauce down the wall. "If I knew that, I'd do something about it."

Buck stared stoically at Skip. "Throwing plates doesn't exactly fix your problem, does it? And it's pretty rude to the hospitality team."

"What do I care? They're paid to clean," Skip scoffed, then saw Buck's face and scrambled to regain position. "Someone is trying to kill me, damnit."

Buck shifted position a little. "So tell me about it," he offered.

Skip scowled. "Okay, why not?" He looked at Megan and patted her on the thigh. "Look, honey, this is business, so you gotta go."

"Aww," she snuggled closer. "I want to stay with you." She patted his shoulder and leaned in. "Help protect you." She wiggled suggestively.

"Look, girl, you can't be here now."

Megan pouted and reluctantly stood up, awkward in her high heels. "Call me." She winked.

"Sure, sure." Skip watched as Megan sashayed out the door. As she closed it, he said, "Women. They don't know when to leave." He rolled his eyes.

Buck said nothing. There really was nothing to say.

"Whatever," Skip exaggerated a sigh. "Look, I was checking into some logs to check when a server went down. My team was screwing it up." He added in a patronizing tone, "You do know what a server is?"

"Go on," Buck growled.

"Okay, okay." Skip's eyes flickered to the right. "There was this repetitive media file upload. Same time every day."

"But that seems pretty normal for a social post?" Buck questioned. "Don't most people schedule them for regular times?"

"Yeah, yeah. But this one, it was the same size file every time. That was weird, so I checked. Same video posted, every day." Skip looked triumphant. "It had been posted five times every weekday for a year."

"Why would someone post the same video every day? What was it?"

"It was some guy fly fishing. Fly fishing! No one posts fly fishing in Blare. Who'd give that a like? Blare is about chill parties, foxy babes, stupendous stuff. Not for the olds. This was the same geezer, doing the same thing, same video. He doesn't even catch a fish, just whacks the water with that string."

"Odd," Buck commented.

"Yeah. So I looked into it. It was the same video and size, but the hash of the file was different," Skip said triumphantly.

"So he's posting fly fishing to his channel every day, then. What's the big deal?"

"No, you don't understand. It looked like the same video, but it wasn't. The files were slightly different every time. So I looked further." Skip was in his element now, interested in the subject and not a bored kid acting out. "Only certain elements were changed, so a code must be embedded in the video, I realized."

"A secret code, huh?" Buck questioned.

"Exactly." Skip ran his fingers through his hair. "I didn't like that. I didn't like that at all. I mean, why wouldn't they just private message whoever they're talking to? That's private enough for almost anything. Blare isn't for spy games. The point is to tell the world what your thing is."

"Probably someone up to something criminal," Buck agreed.

"Yeah. So I thought it'd be a fun challenge to find out what they were up to." Skip shrugged. "I set a couple servers up to hack their algorithm. It took two weeks, but luckily it was pretty basic."

"So what was it?" Buck asked.

"I'm not sure I should give you the details," Skip hesitated.

"It's easier to protect you if I know what's going on," Buck said, interested, despite himself.

"Yeah," Skip thought a minute. "It's like this. Broadly, they're manipulating the stock market. Huge buys or sales of specific stocks, all coordinated. I've counted at least ten different times that it moved a specific stock a billion dollars. A billion freaking dollars." He winced. "Hiding behind my company and stealing that kind of dough."

"That's a lot of money."

"Yeah. I played their system for a few weeks." He winked cockily at Buck. "Had to make sure it's for real, you know?"

"I see."

"After I made a few millions, I decided this business could wreck my company." He shook his head regretfully. "Sometimes you gotta just walk away, no matter how good it seems. Keep your eye on the big picture. Eventually the SEC was going to catch up with them—I didn't want to lose my company when that shit went down."

Buck just looked at him and Skip's eyes shifted uncomfortably.

"So I try to do the right thing. I call the feds, report them." He rolled his eyes. "They told me not to delete the account, let them catch the crooks, so I give them access."

"Sounds like the right move."

"They ask to talk with me in person, speak personally with their tech people. Like anyone speaks in person anymore." He shrugged. "Anyway, I said okay. I mean, I want to stay on the fed's good side, right?"

Buck nodded agreement.

"I fly into KRIC, at Richmond. So they send this lousy car for me. My car's headed to the meeting and the bridge is closed, signs up everywhere. Detours me way out of the route. Driver just follows the signs." He repeated in ominous tones, "The bridge is closed."

"Pretty normal for DC," Buck commented. "A road not under construction, now that would be unusual."

"Well, this time was different," Skip said petulantly. "The detour waved my car," he emphasized, "only my car, down this side street past this creepy van and nothing else. No other cars on the road."

"So what'd you do?"

"I told my driver to keep driving. He started to stop, so I jumped out and hared it for the Metro. Went straight to the airport and onto my plane. I was lucky to make it there alive. I swear I saw like three people following me in the subway."

"I see," Buck kept a straight face. "Did you contact your handlers after that?"

"Yeah, they told me to come here, to the island, instead. Get out of the United States until they knew who could be trusted. Said someone must have leaked the info." He shrugged. "I sure wasn't going back to DC, so the Bahamas was as good a place as any. They told me to go to this island. Controlled access so they could guard me with trustworthy people."

Buck nodded. "An island is about as controlled access as you get. And this island in particular doesn't have a lot of unknowns docking here."

"So I told Jeb and Bud to meet me here. I wanted people I could trust around me—I've known them forever. Jeb flew the helicopter to the airport, so we'd have it if we needed a quick escape."

"That's an idea," Buck said. "And the Smiths?"

"They're not really Mr. and Mrs. Smith," Skip confided with a snicker.

"I get that," Buck said patiently. "They met you here?"

"Yeah, Charlie met me at the airport and flew in with me. Amy rented a boat, so we'd have more maneuverability." Skip stood up and started pacing. "I felt a lot safer with them here, until this murder. I gave all the info to Charlie. I was just holing up here until they gave me the all clear."

"I can see why you wouldn't want to be in public right now," Buck said soothingly. He waited a beat. "So did you ever identify the video poster?"

"Yeah, that was pretty easy," Skip bragged. "He used a bunch of spoof addresses, but once you have the real IP, it's not hard to track. A New York hedge fund. Pretty obvious why they'd want to game the market," he laughed.

"Anyone on the island affiliated with them?"

"If I knew that, I wouldn't need your help, now would I?"

"I guess not," Buck said flatly. "Okay, so the first thing we need to do is move you to a more defensible position in the main hotel."

"Screw that," Skip ejaculated. "I don't want to be next to all those other people. I paid to stay in a cottage and I'm staying here. I want to be isolated so I can see them coming." He made finger shooting gestures. "Bang!"

Buck sincerely hoped the kid hadn't smuggled a gun through customs. He sighed in exasperation. "With a decent team, the cottage would be ideal. Right now, you're isolated and extremely vulnerable. Your perimeter isn't under surveillance. It's the jungle. Anyone can walk by or hide in the bushes—and have easy access to the cottage.

It's simply not possible to guard anyone here under these circumstances."

"I'm not leaving," Skip said, looking out the window at the dimming light from the coming storm. "Except to get off the island."

"Fine by me," Buck said, taking a few steps toward the door. "I only have two security guards on the island. I can't move them from the main hotel area just for you after a murder has been discovered, so I can't offer you any protection out here." He shrugged. "Nothing I can do about it."

Skip threatened, running his hands through his tufts of hair, "If I get murdered on this island, no one will ever come here again." He glared triumphantly at Buck.

Buck rejoined evenly, "On the contrary, if a rich party kid gets murdered, everyone will want to see where it happened. They'll probably post it all over your Blare app. It'd be great advertising for the hotel, as long as we catch the killer. Of course, that won't much matter to you by then." He stared Skip down, his eyes flint. "You know it's true."

Skip's eyes shifted from the big picture windows to the flimsy wood door. He had nothing more to say.

Buck made arrangements with Evie to move Skip to the main hotel, with an adjoining room for the Smiths. Someone was going to get a very nice room upgrade to a cottage, he thought. After it was cleaned.

"Call the Smiths and have them meet us here. Then pack your bags," he ordered Skip.

"I told you, they're not really the Smiths," Skip whined impotently.

Truthfully, Buck didn't know whether Skip was exaggerating the whole affair out of proportion or not. The DC bridge story, where Skip had seemingly panicked over a completely normal traffic situation, made him inclined to think it wasn't likely Skip was under any threat. And even if he was a target, there wasn't any evidence tying the murder of an unknown man on this island to Skip's problems back in the USA.

On the other hand, two federal agents sent along to handle him sounded serious—or two agents who wrangled a resort holiday on the taxpayers' dime. Either way, Buck was going to treat the situation as a potential assassination attempt, until he knew one way or the other.

Despite what he'd told Skip, Mia would not like another murder in her hotel. And neither would he.

The ersatz Smiths arrived promptly after Buck planned the relocation. The male agent was a handsome man, styled dark hair and jaw brushed with five o'clock shadow. "Charlie Smith," he held out his smooth hand to Buck. "Glad you talked sense into the kid. I couldn't believe it when he chose the most isolated place on the island to stay." He shook his head. "It had to be the fanciest place for that kid. Nothing less than the best would do."

"Buck Jaeger." They shook firmly, assessing each other like two boxers in a ring. "I've moved your room to the adjoining guest room."

"As long as this one has two beds," Amy Smith added. "As long as our cover's blown, I might as well sleep comfortably." She scowled at her partner. "I haven't had a good night's sleep since we got here."

"I don't know that your cover is blown to the assassin," Buck told her. "I also don't know that the murdered man we found has anything at all to do with Skip Wilson. His death is probably completely unconnected."

"That's what Detective Albury said when we requested moving Skip off the island," Charlie agreed easily. "Not happening until we find out who the body is, at least. I doubt it has anything to do with the kid. Probably some local drug dealer dumped in the drink." He added with cocky self assurance, "Of course, we'll treat the murder as a threat to Skip until we know for certain."

"It might take a while to get an id, since there's not much to go on. His face and fingerprints were badly damaged by his time in the sea," Buck grimaced. "Not sure how they're going to identify him with so little to go on."

"It's a great place to be stuck, at least," Amy said with a shrug. "Spa day at the government's expense is my kind of job."

"Absolutely," Charlie said. "Though make it diving for me. Of course, the fun's all over if we're on guard duty 24 / 7."

"You dived for long?" Buck knew Charlie had been diving at least once this trip.

"I did some diving in the military, but that was a long time ago. It's been years since I went on a serious dive," Charlie admitted. "Lugged along my antique equipment too, when I heard we were coming here. Took one look at your dive shop and decided I'd rent an upgrade."

"Best thing to do," Buck agreed. "You can't trust old equipment with your life. We'll try to work some dive time in for you once we have these issues contained." He cleared his throat as Skip and the other two entered the room. "Ready to move? Where's your luggage?"

"That's the maid's job," Skip sneered. "I don't haul bags."

Buck told him flatly, "So who's going to go through it to make sure it doesn't have a bomb in it, after it's sat here alone? It's not going to be me, I'll tell you that right now." He emphasized, "And it's not going to be in my hotel. You can get blown up somewhere where it's easy to clean up the mess."

Skip's mouth dropped open.

Amy sniggered.

"Anything you want for the next two days, have it in the bag you're carrying. One bag only. Everyone lugs their own baggage. The rest will go into storage until you leave, but have it packed and ready to go. This cottage is going to the nice people who gave up their room for you."

"You mean the people who got my bougie room in return for their—" he broke off when he saw Buck's face. "Fine!" Skip dragged himself toward his room door.

"So who's going to search them then?" Amy asked, clearly expecting the dirty work would be assigned to her.

"Not my problem," Buck stated. "Hopefully we'll have the murderer in custody by then and they won't have anything to do with Skip Wilson. I'll lock them up in baggage storage for now. Plenty of people leave their dive gear here when they're making a few trips in a season." He was going to search the bags himself before locking them up inside his hotel, but he wasn't about to let Skip know that.

The three young men, to use that term loosely, returned with one bag each, bulging with gaming equipment and t-shirts.

"I still don't see why you're making us move," Skip whined. "I don't want to stay in with the peasants."

Buck ignored him. "I'll lead, you two flank the kids."

"The kids?" Skip protested.

"Act like one, get called one." Buck stated, motioning to the Smiths. "Grow up." As he opened the door, a few heavy drops of rain fell from the gray sky. He pulled up his hood.

"You're making me move in the rain? I'm going to wreck this place on Blare," Skip threatened with a wicked twist of his lips.

"Oh, smart, threaten the guy who's trying to keep someone from killing us," the usually subservient Jeb told him. "Know when to shut up and say thank you, Skip."

"I'd be grateful if people knew it wasn't your sort of party place," Buck told him. "Keeps out the riffraff.

And lies come with lawsuits." He sighed heavily, scanning the bushes around them for movement. "Just act like an adult human being until we get this settled, okay?"

Skip opened his mouth, then shut it.

"I'll tell your mom you moved," Buck offered. "She'll be worried about you, I'm sure."

"Thanks," Skip said dully.

The Smiths quickly moved into place, surrounding the three with practiced ease. Rain started falling harder as they left, drops pattering down around them in increasing frenzy. Heads ducked against the hard onslaught, they moved.

It was a quick journey past the verdant jungle encircling the reclusive cottage to the wide, palm studded path of the main hotel. Buck noticed Charlie remained calm and relaxed, walking with Skip the entire way. Amy Smith was overtly vigilant, militantly striding on the other side of Skip, eyes restlessly scanning and ears pricked for any sign of trouble.

Sandy, in a bright raincoat, passed on a nearby path, trundling her housekeeping cart along and waved cheerfully to them. Amy's jaw clamped down, her dripping ponytail sagged and she continued her march, pointedly avoiding the housekeeper. Charlie nodded shortly to the woman, continuing to try to converse with Skip, clearly trying to keep the young man calm.

Buck hung back a minute, raising his voice over the splashing raindrops, "Sandy, could you wait a few minutes before you clean that cottage?"

She wrinkled her nose. "The sooner that place is done, the better. We don't clean it up, bugs move in." She shook her head, hood wet with rain. "They'll move in fast, in that pigsty."

"I know, I know," Buck held out his hands in supplication. "It's important, trust me. I need to check it out first."

She considered, "I think the new couple took a dive trip. They won't be back for a while."

"That's great, Sandy."

She warned, "I'll need some time cleaning it, so you don't have long." She started moving her covered cart toward the cottages again.

He snorted loudly. "I'll say." He nodded to the little group. "I'll settle them in and get back to it." He jogged to catch up, loping along at an easy pace.

Charlie looked at him quizzically when he returned.

Buck shrugged, "Housekeeping question."

Charlie immediately lost interest, continuing his attempt to calm Skip down. As they entered the hotel, thunder boomed overhead and Skip jumped a foot and gave a high pitched shriek, quickly turning red as guests stared at the dripping group. He glared back, wet hair plastered to his head in straggling strands, revealing just how little hair he had left.

Buck grinned. The kid was really on edge.

The new room was a regular hotel room, much smaller than the cottage, with no sweeping beach views. Raindrops drummed on the window. Those who had rain gear on shed it, raising the humidity in the room considerably.

Almost anyone would be happy with the large beds, comfortable seating area and sparkling marble bathroom. Looking like a drowned rat, Skip glanced around, "This hovel? You expect me to stay here?"

"This hotel room with easy to guard access, yes," Buck told him. "It has no balcony to climb. It can't be entered without going through the lobby where someone is always on duty or the main courtyard, where I've stationed a security guard."

Skip shrugged, resigning himself. "Whatever." He opened his suitcase and pulled out his necessities, console and all. "Someone help me set this up, okay?"

Amy rushed to help.

Buck shrugged. He could have put Skip in a dank, unfinished basement, as long as the kid had his games. If he'd had one, he would have. He checked in with his guard and left to examine the cottage. Sandy's housekeeping cart was parked two cottages down. For all her relaxed and unhurried demeanor, she was the most efficient cleaner at the hotel. Other people would rush around in circles. Sandy never moved fast, but everything was done in the most efficient order in a slow, graceful dance. He knew he didn't have long for his search, as he spied her changing sheets with precision hospital corners two cottages down.

She'd need the time too, Buck thought as he surveyed the destruction of what had been a very nice cottage a few days ago. Moving deliberately, he scanned the room. Probably best to get Sandy to throw out any food in the fridge. Who knew if it had been poisoned?

From the point of view of Skip's nest on the couch, he picked up the coffee table and flipped it over. Well, that was easier than he'd thought, as he removed a tiny microphone. Unfortunately, there was no way to tell who was listening to the bug. It could have been the Smiths or someone interested in learning the latest social media moves. Following time honored tradition, he dunked it in a water glass and continued his search.

8

Flying High

Dr. Sebastian Barbeau and his intern arrived promptly for dinner, looking freshly scrubbed and extremely awkward in the luxurious dining milieu.

Mia greeted them warmly, "Dr. Barbeau, how nice to see you again. And this must be Joshua, your intern?"

The young man reddened under her attention. "Josh Lee, ma'am," his Adam's apple visibly moving. He wore khakis with a brown leather belt and a blue button down shirt, traditional dinner attire, minus the sport coat that would, no doubt, appear with age and tenure. His bony wrists protruded slightly from his shirt cuffs—he must have outgrown it recently or his mother hadn't visited him here yet.

Dr. Barbeau, however, had a—Mia hesitated to call it style—of his own. His dinner jacket was a neon orange windbreaker, clashing horribly with the rich blues of the restaurant. Beneath it was not the t-shirt forbidden by the restaurant, but a Hawaiian shirt with seemingly every color but orange. Royal blue warmup pants completed his glaring ensemble. He hadn't even bothered to shave his two day stubble to go out to dinner with his benefactor. Mia repressed a visible shudder and avoided noticing his shoes. "You've dined at Fritters before?"

The hoped for negative came. "No, we don't have time for fancy dinners out. Too busy with my research." He puffed out his cheeks impatiently and surveyed the room with visible condescension.

Mia just couldn't bring herself to encourage him to dine here more. "Well, I imagine you've eaten their delicious food in room service."

"We have," Josh said, with fervent appreciation.

George delivered a selection of appetizers with a flourish and Josh's eyes lit up.

Mia smiled, "Diving is hungry work, isn't it? My boys used to eat everything in sight after a dive."

Josh helped himself enthusiastically to conch fritters, "I'm always starving after a dive, ma'am. The food here is great."

She took a fritter and bit into it. Perfect crunch. She tried one of the split crawfish, delicately picking out the succulent meat with her fork. Delicious. Surf pounded on the ocean rocks outside, rain made soothing rat-a-tat's on the restaurant roof. It felt cozy and warm inside with the beating storm firmly on the outside.

Dr. Barbeau wolfishly shoveled a white fish ceviche in his mouth, barely bothering to taste the delicacy. He looked around hungrily when his bowl was empty, grabbing a coconut bread roll from the silver basket on the table. Still chewing, he asked, "So what did you want to know about my research?"

"Well, Sebastian," Mia avoided looking into his gaping maw, "I wanted a general idea of what you're seeing on the reef. It would be good to know what worked and what did not, for future reef projects."

Dr. Barbeau pursed his lips, clearly wondering what was in it for him.

"Are you planning on building another reef?" Josh asked with interest.

"Not at the moment," Mia smiled. "But we never know what opportunities might come up in the hotel business. And this reef is a personal favorite project of mine. Having you two tell me about how it's going is a great treat for me." Really, she knew Dr. Barbeau was supposed to be a renowned expert on Bahamian marine life, but that knowledge had to be dragged out of him.

Losing interest, Dr. Barbeau crammed another roll in. "I gave you the charts."

"Yes, and they were very interesting. But it's always better to hear what's actually happening on the reef from the researchers themselves. Data only tells part of the story."

Dr. Barbeau eyed the empty crawfish platter with disappointment. "I don't know what I could add. The charts I gave you tell the story."

Mia slogged on, "Well, for instance, are the primary colonizing corals from the fragments we seeded there or another species? That would definitely be important information for future projects."

"Oh, I get it," Dr. Barbeau said. "You want to spend your money where it's been most useful."

Mia nodded.

"Well, some of the corals are from the imported frags, of course, but the majority are from the remnants of the old reef. Big increase in polyps after spawning season."

"They are all native species, so it's difficult to divide the two groups exactly," Josh added, with a glare from his mentor.

Mia nodded again. "Useful to know. So currents and other reef locations would affect colonization quite a bit."

"I'm most interested in more mobile species in my research. Corals don't move much past the larval stage." Dr. Barbeau gazed into space, contemplating the corals. After a minute, he added, "Only if the rock they're latched onto moves, really."

"So you're primarily studying more mobile species?" Mia prompted when he'd clearly lost interest in conversation.

"Yeah, fish, invertebrates, that sort of thing."

"We're seeing a lot of interesting sea slugs," Josh piped up. "Ones we've never seen before."

"She's not interested in sea slugs," Dr. Barbeau shut his intern up sharply. "Echinoderms are much more interesting. And tourists always like the Cheloniidae."

Chastened, Josh returned to his rapt study of his ceviche.

Mia added, "Everything contributes to the whole, naturally. It's the little interactions on a reef that make it what it is."

George placed three plates in front of them with a flourish, "Pan fried lion fish in a creole sauce, with traditional peas n' rice."

Mia looked down at the buttery brown fish with a smile, "Eating the invasive species, George? What a good idea." She took a bite of the flaky white fish with the spicy sauce. "A very good idea."

George moved away, beaming.

Walking back from dinner, Mia noticed Buck striding down the path. "Having fun?" she asked.

"Thanks a lot, Mia," Buck said sarcastically. "I swear, those kids are mentally still age ten."

"They do seem a little immature for their age."

"Skip told me some rigmarole about people chasing him," Buck sighed heavily, "I can't tell if he's making the whole thing up or not."

"He's not making it up," Detective Albury loomed out of the darkness. "I requested the details sent to me and his story checks out."

"Really?" Mia asked with interest.

"Hard to believe, but Skip Wilson did uncover a market rigging group communicating through Blare." He held out a sheaf of papers. "They sent the basics. He's under protective custody and was given multiple depositions. Amy and Charlie Smith are the federal agents assigned to him." He shook his head in disgust.

"Why they came to my island, I don't know. Surely somewhere in the US would be better for their purposes."

"I wish they'd picked somewhere else too," Mia agreed.

"Well, I guess I'd better go get my beauty sleep, then," Buck said. "The feds are watching him right now, but they'll need a break in the morning." He ambled off to his cottage.

Detective Albury told Mia, "I'll be doing the same. Thanks for finding rooms on site for my men and me."

"Not a problem." Mia grimaced, "We had some cancellations."

He assured her, "I'll clear this up as soon as possible."

"I know you will. Good night and sleep well."

Mia paused a moment after the men had left, looking toward the conference center, now dark. Surely it wouldn't hurt to just check whether they'd locked everything up, now, would it?

Keeping to the shadows, she quickly made it to the conference center and used her master key to enter the dark building. She quietly padded down the hall to the room the police were occupying. All silent. She looked both ways and entered stealthily, quietly closing the door behind her.

Her goal, the printer, sat at the far end of the room. Using her phone light to navigate, she quickly threaded through the chair maze and turned it on, printing out the last document again. She held her light up to examine it. Good, it looked like the information about Skip. She tucked it discretely underneath her jacket, locked the doors behind her and ran for her cottage, feeling like a target was printed on her back in the dark night.

When she reached her cottage, she closed and locked the doors and turned on all the lights.

Slowly turning the pages, she saw that Skip had indeed uncovered a market rigging group of vast sums of money. Crooks had been busy, indeed. The typed documents were covered in schoolgirl round cursive addendums, that must be Amy's, with the occasional backwards slanting scrawl of Charlie's notes. They told a bigger picture than market manipulation, adding money laundering of some very dangerous people's funds.

So Skip wasn't exaggerating. There were probably people wanting to kill him, very much so.

Mia sighed. Why had they come to her island?

Closing the hotel room door behind her with a sigh of relief, Amy made her break for freedom. Charlie, completely immersed in his novel, told her to go ahead and take her break before bed, so she'd get some sleep tonight. He'd barely looked up from his book. He obviously thought so little of her abilities he didn't care if she was around or not. Well, she would show him, show all of them, when this whole mess was over.

Skip and his friends were the worst roommates ever, that was for sure. It wasn't like she could sleep before they went to bed—if they ever did. Repetitive drivel blasted through the doorway, even with all three men wearing headphones, glued to the dancing lights of the screen. She couldn't even close her door to shut out their noise—she was supposed to be protecting them. Protecting them! Laughing to herself, she thought she'd never take a bullet for those idiots.

Walking through the sleeping hotel, she nodded to the security guard sitting at the end of the room wing. She could think of at least two ways she could overpower that guard, if she were trying to force her way in Skip's room. Of course, she didn't have to—she had full access to the jerk—such an honor! Shaking her head, she left through the hotel doors.

The ocean air felt cool on her face after the stuffy room. Lifting her face, she looked up into the sparkling night sky. Over her head was clear and bright, no trace of the recent storm remaining. So many stars stretched out endlessly, dots of light as far as she could see, watched by the glowing moon. For a minute, she stood and looked up into the stars, feeling insignificant under the vast night sky.

With a brisk shake of her head, she moved on, carefully making her way down the steps to the sand. Palm fronds and detritus from the storm lay scattered on the beach. The groundskeepers would clean up before most guests were even awake, but for now, she watched the moonlit sand, so she wouldn't trip on storm debris. Once her eyes adjusted to the pale blue moonlight, she made her way easily down the beach to the isolated dive shack.

Shivering a little in the cool air after the storm, Amy tried the door. Locked tight. Shrugging, she sat on the beach and hugged herself, looking up at the stars. Waves softly sang on the sand as they ebbed and flowed back to her feet.

Not even noticing the soft music of the sea at her feet, she waited for her appointment. Her mind drifted to her new life, one with ample money to spend and the whole world to play in. Dreams of luxurious restaurants and glittering hotels, the most opulent of what the world had to offer, all hers for the taking. All she had to do was nothing.

She shivered suddenly. The beach sand lay cold and clammy under her. Standing up, she brushed off the clinging sand and paced along the water edge, staying close to the bulk of the dive shack. She didn't want to miss her appointment.

When her appointment came, she never even heard the quiet footsteps approaching. She fell hard on the damp sand, her eyes gazing sightlessly at the bright stars. The tide washed her feet, singing sadly.

Sandra had just tucked her bag under her desk and started checking messages from the night concierge when Pete, one of the groundskeepers, ran inside, yelling, "There's a body on the beach!"

Sandra stood up abruptly, feeling the world spin. "Another body?"

"On the beach!" Pete repeated. "WhatdoIdo?" came out in a rush.

"Oh, muddasick!" Sandra swayed hard, holding on to her desk. The hard reality of the wood under her clenched hands felt like the only stable thing in the world for a minute. She closed her eyes for a minute, keeping the churning in her stomach down.

"What do I do?" Pete demanded again. His dark skin was white and eyes wide in shock.

Sandra opened her eyes decisively. This was her job and she would do it right. She didn't have time to faint now. She could always faint later. "Don't go near the body, but cordon off the beach, so no one can see it close. We don't want guests anywhere near it."

Pete nodded, still breathing hard.

"I'll call the police." Sandra told him. "And Evie."

Pete added, "And Ms. Mia, she'll want to know."

Sandra put her hand to her bright pink headscarf. "She will, indeed. I'll call her too."

Pete reluctantly turned to go.

"Pete," Sandra called him back. "Who is it?"

Pete turned back, eyes grim. "A woman." He clarified when he saw Sandra's horror that it might be someone she knew, "One of the guests. I dunno her name."

Sandra felt air reenter her lungs sharply. "Thanks, Pete." She picked up the phone.

Buck abruptly woke with the phone call. It had been a long night. His security guard gave him the bad news. "I figured she'd returned to her old room when she didn't come back."

"Not your fault, Tom. Just keep guests away from the police area." Buck grimaced as he hung up the phone. A second murder would panic guests. They'd be fighting to get off the island. He dressed as quickly as he could and beat it for the lobby.

As soon as she saw him, relief spread across Sandra's tense face. She blurted out, "Pete found her." Buck nodded. Her chalky grey face peeked out under her pink headscarf, her normally vibrant color and smile dulled. "They've cordoned off that area of the beach and the police are on their way."

Buck looked around at a few straggling guests assembling for early breakfast. "There's no hiding this. As soon as guests want to go to the beach, they'll know all about it. Then they'll want to leave."

Sandra nodded, her lips twisting. "Ms. Mia's on her way."

"Good." Mia could handle the hotel guests. "I'll go tell that group upstairs. They don't know yet."

Sandra made a face. "Sooner they're off our island, the better."

"Don't I wish," Buck said with feeling. He turned and bounded up the guest room wing stairs. He wished Skip and his crowd had never even heard of Spinel Reef. This new death definitely connected the murders to Skip's group. Now, everyone would have to do whatever the police ordered and pick up the pieces afterwards.

His gun held loosely ready in his hand, Charlie opened the door, his eyes still bleary with sleep. "Buck? It's pretty early." He rubbed his eyes.

"We need to talk."

Charlie reluctantly opened the door the rest of the way, standing back for him to enter.

"Get everyone up."

Charlie glanced at Buck's set face, and started toward the other room. "Man, I feel awful." He rubbed his face vigorously, trying to wake up and looked around the room. "I don't see Amy. She must have gone out on one of her early morning runs." He shook his head, then winced, holding a hand to his head. "I didn't even hear her go."

"She's dead," Buck told him flatly. "Killed on the beach, probably last night."

Charlie froze, becoming absolutely still. "Dead? Amy's dead?"

"Dead," Buck repeated. "Police will want to talk with us soon, especially you, since you're her partner."

Charlie found a chair and sat down heavily. "Amy's dead," he whispered. His eyes closed.

While Charlie was processing the news, Buck went into the next room and pulled back the curtains, admitting bright sunlight into the dark cave.

"Hey!" Skip objected. "What's the idea?"

Buck turned on the overhead light for good measure. "Get up. Now."

"I don't have to," Skip told him, putting the pillow over his head.

"Amy's dead," Buck stated. "On the beach. Last night. Murdered."

"She's dead?" a voice questioned from the other bed. Jeb asked, disbelieving, "For real?"

"Very real, yes," Buck told him.

Skip sat straight up, rolling out of bed. "We have to get off this island now. Right now."

"You have to wait and talk to the police," Buck told him patiently.

"Like hell I do," Skip yelled. "The woman supposed to be guarding me was just killed. Killed! I'm not staying here." Charlie emerged in the doorway, still rubbing his face and bleary eyed. "And some bodyguard he is. He didn't even notice his partner was gone!" He pulled on shorts and a t-shirt, grabbed his bag and started shoving stuff in. Then he said, "Screw it. I don't need anything. Just get off murder island." He dropped the bag. "Guys, we're out of here. We'll send for our stuff or buy new."

Buck grabbed his arm. "Steady, there," in a soothing tone. "Getting arrested for leaving a crime scene isn't going to help matters. You're connected with Amy's death. You can't leave without police permission."

"I can deal with that from off the island," Skip told him. "Get your hands off me." He ordered his two sleepy friends, "Let's go!"

Jeb protested, "Skip, we'll need to talk with the police, then we'll leave." He clumsily tied a shoelace wrong and retied it, opening his mouth wide in a massive yawn. He got to his feet slowly, gingerly putting weight on his healing leg.

Bud's eyes widened as he scrambled to his feet and pulled on a shirt, fingers fumbling on the buttons. "I dunno, Skip..." he began weakly. "I don't think it's such a good idea to run away from the police."

"I do," Skip told them forcefully. "We're getting out of here while the getting's good." He opened the door wide. "Leave your stuff. Let's go. We're getting off murder island right now." Skip started striding down the hall without looking back. Jeb and Bud stumbled after him, still protesting weakly.

Buck looked at Charlie and shrugged. "Up to you. You want me to stop them?"

"I dunno," Charlie still didn't look awake. "Whatever."

"Hey, are you all right?" Buck asked sharply, focusing on the agent.

"Just so tired," Charlie mumbled, eyelids half closing over dimmed eyes. He rubbed his face again and mumbled, "Just need coffee."

Buck shook his head firmly. "You need a blood test from the police first. You look like you've been drugged."

"Drugged?" His eyelids drooped. "Can't be drugged. Haven't left the room."

"Huh," Buck picked up the phone, calling down to Sandra. "I need a forensics or medical officer up here immediately. And please tell the police that Skip Wilson and his party are leaving the island right now. Heading for their helicopter." He hung up and turned to Charlie, who'd already sat down and closed his eyes again. "I guess you're not going to make that flight, are you?"

A rasping snore was his only answer. The man sprawled on a chair, legs akimbo and neck at a spine breaking angle.

Buck handed Charlie off to the officer as soon as he appeared, telling him to check for barbiturates. Then he took off after Skip's group at a loping run, weaving his way around milling guests. He could see the three men in the distance, heading straight to their helicopter. Jeb set their speed, with his limping stride. Buck ran faster, trying to catch up with the idiots.

Jeb awkwardly climbed into the cockpit and the other two clambered in behind him, starting to strap in. The engine roared to life with a stuttering sound Buck had heard before from a Sikorsky.

He put on a burst of speed and wedged himself in the door. "You young idiots! You're leaving a crime scene you're involved in!"

"Not my problem," Skip yelled back. "My lawyers can deal with it."

"And you weren't thinking about someone trying to kill you?"

"I'm thinking about that, yeah," Skip yelled back at him. "That's why I'm leaving!"

Buck quickly looked around the small cabin, then shoved his hand under Jeb's seat and pulled out a small black suitcase connected to the helicopter by a snaking black wire. "And you didn't think someone might want you on this helicopter?" Opening it wide, the ticking timer and plastic explosive made their faces turn ashy white. "Get out, you fools!" The three men scrambled out of the helicopter.

Buck took a deep breath, examining the bomb. The timer continued counting down—only three minutes left. The numbers changed inexorably as he stared at it. He'd thought his bomb defusing days were long past. He breathed in, holding his breath. One, two, three, four. Deep exhale, one, two, three, four.

The bomb must have been triggered by the engine turning on, but he still should have time. He hoped he had enough time.

Detective Albury came up behind him. "I've got those three in custody." He paused, looking over Buck's shoulder. "What's the trouble here?"

"Bomb," Buck said briefly.

The detective surveyed the object. "Don't want to cut those wires," he said, pointing to the ones that ran under the helicopter dashboard.

"Nope," Buck agreed calmly. "Got a bomb squad here?"

"I do not," the detective said regretfully. "It would take an hour for them to get here."

"Then I guess it's up to us. Wave everyone back."

Detective Albury stepped back and motioned to his men to move. He immediately returned to Buck's shoulder, ready to help.

Buck looked up briefly to check the crowd was far enough back and noticed Mia dwarfed by her hat, her face sheet white, standing at the front of the crowd. He gave her a broad wink and she did her best to return it with a wavering smile.

Okay, he could do this. Breath out. One. Two. Three. Four.

Teasing the wire out of the plastic explosive, he cautiously removed the blasting cap. He carefully clipped the wire going to the blasting cap. "You see any more connections?" he asked Albury.

"None I can see," the detective answered. "It looks like it's designed to be hidden, but easy to dismantle if perhaps, it wasn't needed after all."

Buck met his eyes briefly. "Don't look at me," he told him.

"I saw you running to get them out."

The two men were quiet for a minute. The timer counted down. Albury watched as the crowd was herded far away.

"No guarantee there's not more explosive connected somewhere," Buck warned him. "You might want to move back too."

"I'm good." Albury added, "Bomb squad is on its way."

Buck nodded. "Figures." He breathed out. One. Two. Three. Four. "So here goes nothing." He pulled the timer off the bomb before it finished its count.

Nothing happened.

The two men gave a collective sigh of relief.

"That's that, then." Buck carefully stepped back. "I think I need a drink."

"It's seven in the morning," Detective Albury objected.

"I'll make it a Bloody Mary, then. Brunch."

"When this job's done, I'll stand you a beer," Albury told him.

"You betcha." Buck reached Mia and gave her a bear hug, swinging her small frame around him. "Good to see you, Mia."

Eyes brimming with tears, she answered, "Absolutely."

Skip and his friends had been firmly herded back into their room, with a police guard stationed outside the door to keep them there. When Buck entered, he was surprised to find the room quiet. The tv sat dark and silent and for once, they weren't glued to their computers. Buck quietly closed the door. "Where's Charlie?"

Skip inclined his head to the other room's door. "In there, sleeping it off." He lay back in his chair as if exhausted.

"Did they find out whether he'd been drugged?"

"I dunno," Skip said, "but I tried to tell him about the helicopter and he just closed his eyes and started snoring. He's not exactly a bodyguard right now." He shook his head in disbelief. "I can't believe a bomb was in my helicopter. We could have been killed. I can't believe we weren't killed."

Jeb added, his words deliberately slowed to where his voice wasn't quavering, "I would have been killed, for sure. That, that thing—" he took a calming breath, "was under my seat. I could have easily started the helicopter without them. Skip's always late. A few minutes after—" he mimed a bomb explosion with jangled fingers. "Dead." He stared into space, his hands hanging limp over his healing leg.

"Amy was killed," Buck said flatly. "Garroted on the beach."

Color drained from Skip's face, leaving a sickly greenish yellow.

Buck added, "Looks like a professional job. So did the bomb."

Grimacing, Skip stood up and paced the room, abruptly turning. "I guess they hired someone."

"The hedge fund you were talking about?"

"Yeah," Skip flopped back on the couch, leaning his head back and looking at the ceiling.

Buck cleared off a chair by shoving everything to the floor and sat down. "If they want to kill you badly enough to hire a professional, they'll keep sending assassins until they succeed." He stared at Skip, frowning.

Skip protested, "Hey..."

Ignoring him, Buck asked curiously, "But why?"

"Why what?"

"Why do they want to kill you?" Skip looked confused, so Buck explained. "You've told your story to the feds. Right?" He tapped his leg, working through a mental checklist.

Skip nodded, "Yeah, I gave Charlie and Amy a signed deposition the first day. Told them everything. They sent it off immediately."

"So the government has your files and your statement. They traced the uploads after the point you told them something was crooked. So why is someone trying to kill you?"

"I'm a witness?" Skip's voice broke high.

"It's not like you physically witnessed anything," Buck added with a shrug. "Everything's logged on your servers, right?" He tapped his leg. "Any computer expert could testify to the same thing."

He looked at Skip. "Did you tell them everything?"

Skip burst out, "Of course I did! Do you think I'm an idiot?" He looked at Buck's considering face. "Don't answer that," he said, sounding exhausted. "I told them everything. Absolutely everything."

The room was absolutely quiet except for the sound of Buck's steady tapping on his leg, still deep in thought. The room felt humid and stuffy, despite the air conditioning. Occasional snores came from Charlie's room, punctuating the silence with broken starts. The smell of fear filled the enclosed space, pouring off the three men in waves.

Bud shifted in his chair, looking at the doors and window uneasily. He continually decided to stand up and pace and, as he moved, collapse inward back into the chair. He didn't even glance at his laptop.

Jeb's long face had grown narrow and tight. His hands hung slack, fingers unmoving and impotent, but his jaw worked steadily, a vein throbbing visibly. He seemed in serious shock.

Buck asked Skip abruptly, "Anyone else want to kill you?"

Skip shook his head in confusion. "I can't think of anyone." His earlier frenetic energy was wearing down. He sat listlessly, waiting for someone to tell him what to do. "I don't think anyone hates me that much."

Bud snorted, "Try every ex-girlfriend he's ever had." With an effort, he pulled himself to his feet and started pacing the room.

"Anyone serious about it?"

Skip tried to shush Bud with a quick hand motion, but Bud kept going, the words spilling out like a dam overflowing. "The girls might hate his guts, but they're probably not going to kill him." He walked a little faster, abruptly turning at the curtain.

"Maybe a disgruntled employee?" Buck suggested.

"Nah, my people love me," Skip dismissed that idea.

"Maybe an ex-employee?"

Bud got in before Skip, "Blare's not been around long. Just two years. Not too many employees have left. Great bonuses."

Skip said slowly, "There was that guy, you know, the one who couldn't code." He sniggered, "He didn't like me much."

"John got a job the week after you fired him," Bud said, still pacing the room like a caged animal. "From what I heard, he couldn't code there either. Nah, it wasn't him."

Bud continued, garrulous in his shock, "Now if I wanted to kill you, I'd slip something into your morning coffee. Maybe rat poison or, or," his brow crinkled and he walked faster, "an opiate. Like Jeb had for painkillers after his accident. I could even sprinkle some of those on top of food. When you fell asleep, I could push you off a cliff." He thought a moment, fingers moving with jittery action. "Or on this island, go off a boat into the deep blue sea. You'd couldn't swim a stroke with Jeb's pills in you."

"Bud, I don't think—" Skip objected sharply, his face white and drawn.

"Or in a beer. You know, I've always thought all those little crimps on a bottle cap would be super easy to fake with pliers." Bud warmed to his theme. "But it wouldn't have to be poison. I could slip into his room, say, when the maid was cleaning the bathroom, and put a bomb under the bed so when he lies down, it goes off. Or in his favorite couch spot. No one else sits there or he gets mad. He flops down, and boom!" He moved faster.

Jeb told him, eyeing Skip uneasily, "Bud, don't you think you better stop?"

"Or you could pretend to be the maid, sprinkle poison on top of his sheets. I saw in this movie how some poisons are absorbed by skin. Or light a candle, filled with arsenic, you know? It'd fill the room with fumes and you'd never wake up!" Bud snapped his fingers like an axe falling.

"Or if you're swimming, I could wait under the water, you know, in scuba gear. Then grab you and hold you under until you drowned." Bud laughed harshly. "It'd be easy. What else?" He strode across the room.

"Stop it!" Skip yelled, his hair standing out in tufts as he yanked on it. "Seriously, dude, that's enough."

Bud looked confused. "I'm just trying to help."

"By telling me all the ways I could be killed?" Skip exploded. "Some help!"

"I've got one," Jeb added, looking at Skip.

"What?" Skip yelled at him.

Jeb added, smirking, "How about your mom, when she finds out you were nearly killed by a bomb and didn't bother to let her know you're okay?"

"Oh no..." Skip's face blanched and he grabbed for his phone.

9

A Long Walk

After the initial rush on the concierge's desk, the island relaxed, unwinding from tightly coiled fear. For those wishing to leave the minute they could escape from the island, there would be an extra ferry at the ready. For those remaining on the island to enjoy their planned vacation, there would be vouchers available for everything from free spa treatments to stays at any one of the Spinel Resorts.

When the guests understood Amy Smith had been one of Skip Wilson's party, anxieties relaxed. There was a feeling that anything might happen to a guest of Skip's, with his controversial Blare empire. As one guest told the concierge, "Someone was bound to get killed around that jackass kid. Too bad it happened on my vacation."

His petite wife chirped in, "But I can't wait to tell the girls when I get back home. No one else had a murder on their vacation."

As the mood of the guests had shifted back to vacation mode, Mia quietly effaced herself, exchanging the humming hotel for the quiet contemplation of the beach. Avoiding even glancing at the police tape cordoned section of beach where Amy's body had been found this morning, Mia strolled in the opposite direction. She warily dodged around the volleyball game, already back in progress, and began walking up the white sand. Answers came easier while walking.

The bomb had scared her, badly. Buck had always dived headlong into danger. It was who he was. Herself, she'd have moved all the people far away from the bomb and cleaned up the mess afterwards. No helicopter—or pristine landing pad—was worth taking even a chance on anyone's life.

Of course, she'd always known Buck took chances. Calculated risks, he'd call them, and he and Leo would laugh over the stories afterwards. They probably were acceptable risks for someone trained in bomb disposal, like Buck. Or someone who'd been through some tough situations in the military, like Leo. They just weren't acceptable risks to her. This situation had to end soon.

Mia paused a moment, looking out to sea. The horizon seemed such a long way off, but she'd been beyond the far blue rim just a few days ago, in Buck's lovely old boat. She'd been worried about her old friend after Sarah died, but he was healing here, on the island.

Islands changed people. They always had.

Each of the Spinel hotels was like its own little island, of course, even the ones not actually located on islands. Everything in the hotel centered on the guests, but guests ebbed and flowed, very few of them affecting the resort team much. Naturally, they'd enjoy having some guests and dread the return of others, but the hotel itself didn't change because of the guests. Hospitality team members tended to stay a long time. Friendships grew and grievances magnified, in isolation from the rest of the world. Small imbalances, little pieces of grit introduced into their smoothly running gears, were felt all the more because of the isolation. Her team was not going to be happy about two murders and a bomb on their island.

Mia couldn't think of much of a way to reassure them except to find the murderer as quickly as possible. So she started thinking furiously, walking slowly on the white sand.

From what Buck had told her, the murderer was either a professional assassin or someone who hated Skip obsessively. While the latter wasn't hard to believe—his utter rudeness to his sweet, conscientious mother was not a trait Mia appreciated—she thought the murder must be a professional job.

Most ordinary people wouldn't know how to make a bomb. She certainly didn't. And it wasn't the sort of thing one would look up online. That sort of question got federal agents asking questions back.

Mia remembered Amy telling her how she'd be retiring soon—on a lot of money. Mia had wondered at the time whether the woman was anticipating the death of a relative to a terminal disease. She'd seemed morbidly giddy about getting that fortune. Amy had been so very sure that she would have money to spend in the near future. Mia guessed now, Amy had indeed been anticipating a death, but that of Skip, not her own.

She remembered Amy arriving on the boat the same day as Skip, hauling all that heavy dive gear while her husband checked out the beach. Except Charlie Smith wasn't her husband at all. The two agents clearly didn't even like each other. They were only working together to guard and interview Skip, not friends or close partners.

Mia was now sure Amy had been feeding information to whoever wanted Skip dead. Poor dead Amy, trading Skip's life for money. Mia shook her head sadly at Amy's choice. Such a waste.

So, who would want information about Skip? That was the only currency Amy had worth trading.

She was sure it was someone on the island. She dismissed the resort team. While possible, they were unlikely. People didn't change jobs very often, here on the island, and there simply weren't any new employees. Someone could have been paid enough for an amateur attempt, but it was unlikely. There was that professional bomb to be considered. No, the simplest explanation was the best—the murderer lurked among the guests.

Amy's confederate had probably been introduced on the island at the same time as Skip. Skip's decision to hide out here had been made at the last minute, with him only booking reservations the day before his arrival. So one of the people arriving that day—and also making reservations then or later—must be a professional killer.

She could ask Evie about later reservations, but that didn't rule out a murderer using the name of a reserved guest. Most people would gladly give up a hotel reservation if offered enough money and it would be difficult to discern actual names without checking everyone's passport. Most of the guests currently on the island had arrived that day, so arrival time wasn't a good clue.

Amy had been garroted quite professionally as well. Unfortunately, a wire had been used, which didn't rule out a female killer. Something that quick and deadly could be done by almost any healthy adult with the element of surprise on their side. Amy had expected a payoff, not a murder. The foolish woman had probably gotten the payoff she deserved.

And the mystery body? It had been found on the deep side of the reef. Now, they knew the killer probably had free access to Amy's boat. He might even have arrived, hidden, on it.

While Mia didn't find any hard evidence in the boats, anyone who knew how to row a dingy could have taken the body out to the reef and cast it into the depths with a concrete block attached to sink it to the ocean floor. Amy, for one, could easily have dumped a body overboard, all by herself.

The forethought behind that concrete block seemed very professional, as well. However, even Mia had read enough mysteries to know that's what the mob did when taking their victims 'sleeping with the fishes.' So that didn't prove anything. Anyone might think of a concrete block and tie it to the body.

However, Mia had actually seen that body on the beach, the body that wasn't supposed to exist. So someone had carried it from hiding, then paused when they heard her coming? When she hurried away for help, quick as a flash, they whisked it out to sea.

Could Amy have done that? Maybe, Mia decided. She'd been in peak training for whatever government agency she worked at. She knew from yoga class and the nature hike that Amy was in excellent physical shape. And all that money and the possibility of a murder trial were prime motivators for hauling something heavy.

Still, Mia hadn't seen drag marks or signs of wheelbarrow wheels. While Amy could certainly have hoisted the man briefly, Mia didn't think she could have carried him very far on her own, not unless she was a weightlifter. Certainly not without traces Buck would have observed. And she already knew there was someone else involved, by the simple fact of Amy's brutal death.

Mia thought it was a man, a strong man, who had lifted that body and carried it to a hiding place and later to a watery grave.

She dismissed Skip's two friends, Jeb and Bud. If they were going to kill Skip, they'd hardly need Amy's help with the project. And they'd been in that helicopter, primed to explode. No, they weren't killers.

As much as she hated to consider it, Carol was a very efficient woman. She seemed to love her son Skip, despite his obvious faults, but children didn't grow up in isolated bubbles. They often developed personalities similar to their parents. Did Skip inherit his self-centeredness from Carol or her ex-husband? Was she depraved enough to kill her own son? She appeared to be a mom struggling to do the best for her son, while still trying to preserve her dignity. Could she be something a lot darker? Mia hoped not, but there was clearly a great deal of money involved. People sometimes did terrible things for money.

A professional, now. Mia walked along, musing. Well, Skip's evidence was all about someone gaming the markets. Donna had mentioned her husband, Todd, had worked for a hedge fund—and still consulted privately. He'd had some meetings while he was here—and their trip was scheduled at the last minute. Mia decided she needed to find out who Todd's meetings were with. Sandy or another resort team member might have noticed Todd entering a room that wasn't his. So he was one possibility and whoever he was meeting with, another.

Who else?

Charlie Smith obviously didn't like his now deceased partner very much. Maybe he realized Amy planned to trade Skip's life for her retirement money. Perhaps he was in on the deal. Or maybe they just didn't get along, Mia thought ruefully. When a murder was involved, it was easy to magnify normal dislikes into murderous hatreds.

One question was why had the group come to the island? It wasn't an obvious choice for an American witness in protective custody. Spinel Reef wasn't that well known a resort. It wasn't typically found in Blare photos —not an elite watering hole with all the glitz and glamour, but a quiet family resort. The hotel was isolated, yes, but wouldn't Amy's killer find it difficult to escape from the island because of that?

Maybe, just maybe the killer was already on the island before Skip and his party arrived. The only temporary resident she could think of was Dr. Sebastian Barbeau and his grad student. No hedge fund manager, he. But Mia believed Dr. Barbeau was the person on those secretive midnight dives.

Could the body be connected with whatever Dr. Barbeau was doing at night on the reef? Perhaps Amy had seen him move the body or something else. Could the murders be about drug trafficking, not Skip Wilson at all?

Amy could have witnessed something completely unconnected. Maybe there was a sunken Spanish galleon with a treasure trove, uncovered by a recent storm. In her mind's eye, Mia saw the rich gold of doubloons glinting from beneath the sand.

A drug deal was much more likely, here on an island. Maybe Amy had seen a handoff during her night surveillance. She might have tried to blackmail the drug dealer and been killed for her trouble. The helicopter bomb could have been separate from the murders—it had such a professional flair to it.

Dr. Barbeau was definitely up to something, she'd stake a good bit on that.

Who else? Mia realized she had been assuming the killer was a man. Two women, Amy and the unknown killer, could have moved the body together, without leaving drag tracks. What about Megan, the recent divorcée, who'd gotten so very cozy with Skip? Being on the prowl for a new man would be an easy way to deflect suspicion. And Megan was not the kind of person wives would invite to dinner.

Mia sighed. There was an entire island full of guests—and suspects. Even not being reasonably fit wasn't a deterrent. For all she knew, Amy could have been knocked over the head before being garroted. And tracks of something to carry the unknown man could have been swept away using fallen palm fronds or splashing water over footprints.

They'd have had to be quick, though. Mia hadn't been gone from the beach for long.

She carefully placed one foot in front of the other, letting her frustration sink into the sand and swirl away with the tide. She needed to think clearly, but her mind felt all snarled up. That bomb, so close to killing Buck, had scared her badly.

"Hi there!" a voice called loudly.

Mia continued walking, concentrating on suspects.

"Hey, Mia! Over here!"

She looked up, startled. "Oh, Henry, hello." She smiled ruefully. "I'm afraid I was puzzling over our problem."

"Two murders," he nodded. "Yes, quite a problem for the island." He waved a hand, "Come up and sit. Two heads are better than one."

Mia navigated her way up the decrepit stairs, trying each for stability before trusting her weight to it. "You know, I could send a man from maintenance to fix these."

"My house, my task," Henry deflected gruffly. "Tea?"

"Yes, please," Mia said politely. Despite the stairs, the porch was neatly swept. Pig greeted her, curly tail waving madly as she snuffled a greeting.

"We can't have murders on this island," Henry said with mock solemnity as he returned with a tea cup. "It upsets Evie." His mouth twitched.

"It upsets me," Mia rejoined.

Under his bushy beard, his face grew serious. "Me too." His brown eyes squinted out over the blue ocean, as if seeing something very far away. "I feel responsible for this place, you know. I don't like the idea of some person terrorizing it."

"No," Mia said thoughtfully. "The island was in your wife's family, you said?"

His eyes blinked hard, determined to look at the horizon. "Yes. She was the last of her family. No one left but me. I wouldn't have sold it, otherwise."

"Are there any tales of Spanish galleons, pirate treasure? Anything of that kind?"

"Enough to kill over, you mean?"

Mia nodded eagerly.

Henry barked a laugh. "It's the Caribbean, you know. Lots of exciting treasure tales. Buried treasure for credulous tourists is a mainstay of the dive boats."

"Any credible ones?"

"Not really." Henry was silent for a minute, his eyes on the blue vastness. "My wife said she picked up a doubloon or two when she was a kid, I think on the island." He shrugged. "Could have been somewhere else, though. Never found enough to matter."

Mia let the sunken treasure theory drop. "It was just an idea."

"Anything's possible," Henry agreed. "But I think when they surveyed for building the reef, they would have found some sign of a sunken ship. It was a very thorough survey." He shrugged again, "But maybe not. It's a big ocean." His eyes flickered to hers, then sought comfort in far away waves.

"You heard about the bomb?" Mia asked.

Henry shuddered, grimacing beneath his beard. "Yeah. At the helipad, right?"

"In the helicopter," Mia corroborated.

He shook his head. "Why anyone would want to arrive on that noisy machine instead of a boat, I don't know."

"It's faster," Mia offered. "That matters to some people."

"But, man, speeding through vacation? Why would it matter then?" Henry shook his head. "That kid arriving with his whole retinue in tow. Even his mom, right?"

Mia nodded.

"Hiring his mom as a CFO instead of letting her enjoy early retirement. Crazy." Henry petted Pig, who squirmed beneath his hand. "That pilot didn't know what he was doing when he landed. Almost whipped the tail around, he was so wobbly."

"One of Skip's friends. Apparently a new pilot."

"I could tell," Henry agreed. "It's a good thing that fed was with them. I expect he could have flown in any real trouble. He looks like the sort that would have had some pilot training." He propped his feet up on the railing and took a long drink from his mug.

Surprised, Mia asked, "Charlie Smith flew in?" Somehow she thought he'd arrived on Amy's rental boat, with Amy.

"Sure, I saw him arrive," Henry told her. "Looks a lot better without that beard, too." His hand massaged his straggling beard. "I'm going to have to shave mine off soon," he said. "It's really too hot for a beard here."

"It is that," Mia said absently. "Are you sure the bearded man on the helicopter was Charlie Smith?"

He looked at her and smiled. "Still hunting for your bearded man, huh? Wasn't finding his body enough for you?"

"He didn't fly in from outer space," Mia said with acerbity. "He had to get on the island from somewhere."

"Well, it wasn't by helicopter," Henry said definitively. "That was Charlie."

Mia wasn't so sure, but she knew how to find out.

Mia knocked on the door of Skip's hideout. After a slight pause, Buck opened it fully. "Come to see the troublemakers?"

"Hey!" Skip protested, not very forcefully. "Is it my fault someone's trying to kill me?" he whined.

"I don't know," Buck returned, narrowing his eyes at him. "Is it?"

Skip glared back, then dropped his eyes. His head returned limply back to his hands. Staring at the wall, he ran his fingers through his thinning tufts of hair.

Bud was curled up on the corner of the sofa, fast asleep and softly snoring. Buck nodded at him benevolently, "Shock. Takes some like that."

"Some bodyguard he is," Skip sneered.

"Yeah, you got your friends mixed up in some big trouble," Buck told him. "They've really had your back on this and done their best to help. You should have hired a team, not dragged them into your mess."

Skip looked down at the floor.

Jeb's long narrow face drawn with stress and pain, "So we're all still here. Still alive so far."

"So I see," she said tartly. She nodded to the closed door, "Is Charlie Smith still there too?"

"Yeah, he's pretty dopey still, so we're leaving him alone," Buck told her. "The docs said he was slipped a mega dose of regular sleeping pills, so no point in moving him. He's just sleeping it off." He shrugged, "It'll be out of his system, so he'll be some help soon, I hope."

"I bet Amy gave him those pills," Skip added. "I always knew there was something wrong about her."

"Did you now?" Buck asked softly.

Skip quit talking.

"Well, I have a question for you all," Mia said.

"Yes, ma'am?" Jeb said.

"Did Charlie Smith arrive by helicopter with you? At the same time?"

Jeb frowned. "Of course he did. He met us at the airport and escorted us to the island."

"Couldn't exactly do that without being in the helicopter, could he?" Skip added sarcastically.

"That makes sense," Mia agreed. "Did he wave a sign with your name at the airport? Page you? How did he find your group? It's not that small an airport and you hadn't met in person," she asked curiously.

Skip blew out a long sigh, puffing his hair up like a dandelion. "Everyone knows what I look like." He was clearly regaining his annoying attitude quickly. "He came up to us. They'd sent me a photo of the agents, Amy and Charlie, told me to expect them at the airport. Charlie looked like the photo they sent, stupid retro beard and all. Amy looked a lot hotter in her photo than in real life, but we didn't meet her until we got to the island—she was getting the boat in case we needed it."

"I see," Mia said. "Well, if there's anything you all need, just ring the concierge."

"Just to get off this miserable island," Skip told her. "And never come back again."

Mia held her tongue. That was what she wanted too.

"Detective Albury asked me to give this paperwork to Mr. Smith, since I was coming this way," Mia told Buck. "He needs a response."

"Sending you on his errands, huh? I'll see if he's up to it." Buck tapped lightly on the door and entered, then waved her in.

Charlie Smith was lying down, propped up on pillows and aimlessly clicking through channels. He looked pale and groggy, only half awake.

Mia handed them the sheaf of papers Albury had given her. "Are you feeling better, Mr. Smith?" He didn't look better. His skin was pasty white under his tan and he had dark purple circles, almost like bruises, bagging his eyes.

He smiled wanly, making an obvious effort to appear alert. "Call me Charlie, Mrs. Spinel. My last name's not really Smith."

"I know. Charlie, then." She smiled back and thoughtfully handed him a pen. "Detective Albury wanted your sign off on that," she said, her eyes discretely scanning the paperwork as he removed it from a yellow envelope. "Your office is sending someone to facilitate the transport of Amy Smith's body tomorrow, I think."

He scanned the pages briefly, tapping the pen in his right hand. "That'll work," he said in general. He made a few notes on the cover sheet, then handed it back to Mia, keeping the rest of the paperwork to look through. "Thanks for messaging this. It's good to know her body will be taken care of soon."

"No problem, I was checking on Buck anyway," Mia said mendaciously. "I think Detective Albury is a little short of manpower. It's not as if he can pull every policeman off the mainland and bring them here," she forced a slight chuckle.

"I guess not," Charlie agreed. "Well, he's doing the best he can, as are we all."

"Yes, indeed. I hope you're feeling better soon."

"I'm sure I will once that stuff wears off." As she left, he was already settling back into the pillows, restlessly clicking through another channel.

Buck ushered her out the door. "Still looking for your bearded man, huh?" he asked her. "Mia, you found the body. You're right; he was there. I was a jackass and completely wrong. Can't you just let it go, now?"

"I can't discover how he got on the island," Mia told him plaintively. "But I guess he wasn't the bearded man in the helicopter, since everyone that says that was Charlie."

Buck looked at her seriously, "Leave it to the police, Mia. Murder and bombs aren't a joke."

"No, I know that," she agreed. "I think I'll have a nice dinner and go to bed early." She looked up at his tall, handsome frame with her bright blue eyes. "Don't you worry about me. I'm fine."

Buck sighed heavily and tapped on the wall, "At some point, I really do have to talk to Mark."

"And tell him what?" Mia asked, with asperity. "Don't bother him right now, when things are coming to a head. Detective Albury is doing just fine," Mia told him. "Don't worry about me. This will be over soon."

She trotted down the hall at a faster pace than normal, feeling his eyes boring into her back.

10

At Sea

T hinking furiously while walking through the lobby, Mia almost ran into Carol. She was heading in the direction of Skip's room, a tall frosty glass in her hand.

"Oops, I'm sorry!" as Carol neatly grabbed her drink out of the air. "Oh, hi, Mia. You hear about my son nearly getting killed? Killed!" her voice rang shrilly, quavering on the higher registers. She wasn't exactly tipsy, but had clearly downed a previous drink after the shock of her son's helicopter bomb.

"I heard," Mia told her compassionately. "Are you okay?"

Carol looked at her blankly for a minute, then quietly started crying. Tears ran down her face, tracing lines through the powder of minimal makeup she wore. Mia quickly shepherded the mother to a quiet corner. "Am I okay?" Carol repeated, then laughed a little hysterically, more tears streaming down her face. "Oh, God. I don't know what I am."

Mia told her softly, "You're grateful your son's alive. And you're mad at him for almost getting killed." She patted her shoulder, sympathy in her eyes.

Carol stared at her, then slowly stopped her tears. "That's it exactly." She smiled halfheartedly, wiping her eyes with a quick swipe. "I remember when he tried that stupid skateboard stunt and ended up with a broken arm. I was so glad he was okay, it wasn't worse, but furious with him at the same time."

"And there speaks the mom of a boy," Mia smiled gently.

Carol patted her face with a tissue. "I don't know what to do next. This is a lot bigger mess than a silly skateboard accident."

"You're his mom. All kids get in stupid positions sometimes. We love them anyhow and try our best to extricate them." She smiled. "Just tell him you love him."

"I do, so much," Carol hiccuped a little and a tear ran down her face. She quickly wiped it dry and swept her hand through her short brown hair, fluffing it like soft feathers.

Mia continued, "Of course, as moms, our job is to call them on the stupid, too."

Carol thoughtfully nodded and took a fortifying swig of her frosty drink. "You're right. All his quick success has gone straight to his head. He needs to know he makes mistakes, just like everyone else. From what he's told me after the accident, he made a big one."

"He's got some good friends up there, if he starts letting them tell him home truths. Surrounding yourself only with sycophants is never a wise idea for anyone."

"No, it's not." Carol placed her drink on the table and stood up, stretching her lean athletic frame a little. "He's got to learn that sometime. Now would be a good time to start." She smiled dourly and strode toward her son.

Mia walked down the length of the dive dock, looking at the clear water. The day was warm, with a tranquil breeze out on the end of the dock. Fish swam by, bright jewels shining in the turquoise water. She watched them for a minute, then noticed divers in dark wetsuits below.

The two divers swam slowly, examining every inch of the sandy bottom. It must be Dr. Barbeau and Josh. They took notes on a white clipboard, writing underwater with a neon yellow pen. One pointed ahead, and Mia saw them circling a small emerald green creature, outlined in shocking orange, moving slowly toward the reef. The two scientists followed it, taking notes rapidly as they measured it, holding out a ruler from a discrete distance away. A camera flashed multiple times underwater, taking photos from every conceivable angle. The brightly colored animal kept moving steadily away, as if determined to escape the scientists. Eventually they let it swim off, motioning to each other exaggerated thumbs ups.

The two swam to the dock ladder and swarmed up. Mia greeted them cheerfully, "Hi, you two! Working hard, I see."

Josh swung his tank off, letting the heavy weight gently slide to the dock. "Hi, Ms. Mia! You wouldn't believe how close we got this time!"

Mia noticed Dr. Barbeau was making hushing motions, to no avail, since Josh wasn't looking in his direction.

He burbled, "That's at least ten separate individuals of that nudibranch we've documented. We have a new species! A new species!"

Dr. Barbeau slumped, defeated. He thumped his tank down to the dock. "Josh, I told you..."

"But she's the hotel owner, not a scientist," Josh burbled. "Surely—" he froze as he saw his boss's face.

"What's this?" Mia asked, in measured, ominous tones.

Dr. Barbeau slumped a little more, his tanned chest going concave inside the slick wetsuit. "A new species," he explained unwillingly. "We've discovered a new species on the reef."

"A new species? But that's wonderful!" Mia exclaimed. "That's just what we're hoping for!"

"A sacoglossan," dragged out of Dr. Barbeau.

"That's a sea slug," piped up Josh. "Never seen it before and can't find it in the literature." He danced a little jig.

"That little emerald green creature?" Mia asked. "That was gorgeous," she enthused, slightly over the top for a slug.

"The green comes from the algae it eats, then uses for photosynthesis," Dr. Barbeau added. "So it gets some of its energy from sunlight."

"A creature with its own built-in solar panels, then? How fascinating," Mia told them.

"I'm trying to keep it a secret," Dr. Barbeau said, his brows furrowing. "Until I publish our find, that is." He told her seriously, "I don't want all the molluscan biologists flocking to steal my discovery."

"No, of course not," Mia agreed, keeping her face straight. "Science is a publish or perish world."

He looked at her with pleading brown eyes, "Would you mind?" his voice cracked and he coughed.

"Yes?"

"Would you mind, I mean, I know it's your reef, but could I?" his lips compressed with emotion.

"Yes, Dr. Barbeau?"

"Could I name it after my mother?" burst out like water from a dam. "Because it's beautiful."

"Oh, I see," Mia hid her smile. "Well, it's not completely up to me, of course, but I don't see why not." This vibrant new sea slug was interesting, and definitely something to put in their dive brochures, but not something she particularly wanted the Spinel name attached to. And it seemed to mean a lot to Dr. Barbeau, undoubtably a thoughtful son, bringing his mom a named sea slug, instead of a macaroni decorated card.

He fervently grasped her hand in his wet one and gave hers a heartfelt shake. "Thank you," he choked out. "It means so much to me to—so much."

Mia coughed. "I'm sure your mother will be very proud." She coughed again. "I'd love you to tell me all about it," or at least the highlights, she privately thought. "And maybe point one out on a dive, if we can find one?"

"Oh, I'll find you one! Don't worry about that," Dr. Barbeau swung her around and hugged her, damp as he was. "Oh, Mom's going to love the *Elysia Sylvia*!" His proud grin spanned his face.

After the champagne had been popped in celebration with the two scientists, Mia sat alone at the balcony table, looking out to sea. Josh and Dr. Barbeau had hurried off after toasting the slug, and as happy as she was at their discovery, Mia had not felt inclined to ask them to join her for dinner a second night in a row.

She sipped her champagne, enjoying the fizz of cool crisp bubbles on her tongue. Everything was calm now, a little before the evening rush. The air felt warm on her skin. The sun lay low on the horizon, but the sky was still a pale blue, tinged with faint green on the edges. A peaceful, quiet time.

The little harbor was quiescent, boats gently bobbing in the ebb and flow of the tide. Day sailors had returned from their fishing or scuba adventures and headed for their rooms to wash the salt spray off before dinner. No one was moving around the docks or beach. The only place bustling on the island during this down time were the kitchens, preparing the nightly feast. Out here, looking across the docks, all was calm, waiting. Waiting.

Mia sipped her champagne, nibbled a roll spread with a local goat cheese, and felt her heart slowly beating in her chest. She didn't know if the killer would flee now or wait until two in the morning. If they waited until late evening even, the chances of them being discovered went up astronomically. So she was betting on the killer fleeing now, before watching guests came out to dinner. Guests and waiters would notice the killer fleeing then. Now, they could just slip away.

George paused a moment by her table, on his way to Fritters, "You're a bit early tonight, aren't you, Ms. Mia? Everything okay?"

"Everything's fine. I'm just enjoying the sunset," Mia reassured him. "Take a seat for a minute."

He held up his left arm, checking his watch. "I've got a few minutes." He sat down, stretching out his long legs with a long sigh. "Nice out here in the evening."

"It is." Mia sipped her champagne. "I've been meaning to have a little chat with you, George."

"Uh oh," he said with mock dismay. "What is it this time?"

"It's about time you settled down, you know," Mia told him frankly.

He held up his hands, laughing. "Mia, now, don't you try that one on me. You've got two sons and a daughter to matchmake."

"But George," she remonstrated. She was only trying to help.

"I know Sandy's the girl for me. I don't need you to tell me that." He looked at her with a definite smirk curving his lips.

"Then hurry it up," she told him tartly. "I'm only on the island a few weeks."

"Like you wouldn't come back for my wedding." George chuckled and got to his feet, patting her shoulder with his strong hand. "Thanks, Mia. It means a lot, that you think so too."

After he left, she sipped her wine and nibbled her snack, planning beachfront weddings and wondering what hotel George would like for his honeymoon. Of course, it was really the bride's choice, so she'd have to have a talk with Sandy soon. After George asked her, of course.

The sun slowly sunk towards the distant water, sending faint pink trails into the sky. An elderly couple ambled out, commanding a beachfront table. She watched them slowly settle at the table, admiring the sunset. Elizabeth served them dinner rolls and left, finishing preparing her station for the evening rush. The couple were thankfully quiet, perusing their menus.

Mia sighed and finished her glass with disappointment. She wasn't particularly hungry right now. She'd expected the killer to try to escape now, but they hadn't. Maybe she was wrong. She started reviewing the clues in her head, checking the points off, one by one.

The corpse on the beach had a beard, but no bearded man fitting that description had been on the island. Only one bearded man with that description had arrived on the island—and he had flown in by helicopter and no longer had a beard of any kind.

The watch she had found near the reef had really set her on the right track. The still shiny watch was obviously a precious memento from a loved one, but no one had reported it missing. With scratches all along the left side of the dial, it must have been worn by a left handed man on his right hand. There might be other reasons for wearing a watch on your right hand, but left handedness was the most common. Mia thought the watch must have belonged to the dead man—anyone else would have complained to the concierge about losing their watch, hoping someone would find it and return their cherished piece. So the dead man was left handed.

There was one person at the hotel who had left handed signatures on documents and a right handed signature in person. And here he was, right on schedule.

Charlie—not Smith and probably not Charlie—loped around the side of the building, moving fast in the grey dusk. He headed straight for the dock, going to the far end, where Amy had berthed their boat. He jumped aboard with a catlike leap and started the engine in a soft put-putting, trolling along as he slowly swung out of the harbor, making as little noise as possible.

Mia sighed with relief that the ordeal was almost off her island.

Calling Buck, she told him in carefully modulated tones, "The man calling himself Charlie Smith just took Amy's boat. He's leaving the island right now. Escaping justice, if I'm not mistaken."

"What? Charlie's in his room," Buck mumbled, evidently awakened from a sound sleep. "His turn on watch."

"That man's no federal agent."

"What?"

"He's a fake, masquerading as the real federal agent. The real agent was the dead man I found. And the killer's leaving the island right now," Mia's voice was edgy.

Then, "What! Leaving the island?"

"As we speak. Headed southwest, toward the mainland."

"Not on my watch!" He clicked off, already yelling something to a listener.

Mia next called Detective Albury, who picked up on the first ring. "Charlie Smith is leaving the island in a boat, right now. I believe he is the murderer and attempting escape."

"Is he now?" Detective Albury said in clipped tones. "He won't get far." He hung up.

Mia smiled in satisfaction, watching the boat spray start flying in the distance, as Charlie decided he was far enough to risk engine noise. Behind her, she heard running as Buck, dragging Jeb in nothing but pajama pants with little helicopters on them, ran for the helicopter. Detective Albury wasn't far behind, two police officers in tow, jumping on the police boat. They sped out with a loud roar of the engine. All the harbor boats strained their lines, thudding furiously in the strong wake.

The hard whomp of helicopter blades cut the air. Mia saw Jeb's intent white face frowning in concentration as they flew by. Buck leaned out, pointing to the boat ahead, motioning to the police boat below. The helicopter skimmed the water, moving fast, barely over the waves. They quickly approached the boat and Buck leapt as the helicopter veered off.

As Buck leapt out of the helicopter, Charlie swung away from the wheel and the boat floundered against the current. He shot wildly, emptying his chamber in Buck's direction, but missed as the boat lurched through the waves. One bullet grazed Buck's shoulder slightly, but his adrenaline was pumping too fast for him to care. He pounced on Charlie, decking him in one easy movement. His useless gun bounced on the deck.

Charlie rolled up, moving like a cat, and pulled a wickedly sharp hunting knife out of a leather sheath hidden beneath his shirt. "Why did you come after me, old man? Now I have to kill you too."

"Why'd you come to my island?" Buck lunged and missed.

Charlie swiped at him with his hunting knife, tearing Buck's shirt, but not his skin. "Easy location, in and out. Bunch of retiree has beens, like you."

"You're caught in a trap now, you fool."

Charlie's eyes flickered, finally seeing the police boat catching up, now that no one was at the wheel. The boat swung wildly around, seesawing from crest to crest.

Buck moved during that brief moment, tackling him down to the deck. But Charlie wiggled like an eel as the boat surged through a wave, rolling to the side and out of Buck's grasp. Both men were flung against the gunnels, staggering to remain upright.

Buck heard Jeb circling him in the helicopter, rotors beating the air. He didn't know why the kid was still there—it wasn't as if he could do anything from the air. He watched Charlie, dark eyes darting as he panted, tensing for an attack.

Charlie eyed the police boat closing in on them, knowing he was running out of time to get away. He had to make a move soon, or lose his chance. His boat was bigger and faster. He could outrun the police, but he had to get away now. He was out of time.

Charlie suddenly lunged at Buck, leaping across the deck like a cat. His face twisted in a snarl and his knife was out, ready to gut Buck. Diving to the side, Buck twisted around to tackle his attacker. He slammed the knife hand down again and again until the knife dropped and slid across the deck.

He kept his body weight flattening Charlie until he felt the bump of the police boat. The boat swayed as Detective Albury jumped on board, quickly clipping handcuffs on the murderer.

Beach Party

Mia let her white silk wrap drop elegantly to her shoulders as she entered the banquet hall to burbles of happy chattering. French doors opened wide to the sound of soft ocean waves caressing the beach. It had been a beautiful ceremony on the beach. Evie bustled over as she entered, laughing and radiant, in layers of shimmering white chiffon, looking like she was dressed in an elegant meringue. "Mia! You need to tell this silly man pigs are not allowed in my restaurants." She placed one round hand on her hips, hidden beneath the frothy fabric.

Henry stood smiling down at her, pale skin showing where his wild beard had been, Pig at his side. "Evie, this isn't one of your restaurants. It's a banquet hall and open to all the elements." Pig leaned in toward Evie, small dark eyes pleading.

"There's food in here!" She threw up her hands in disgust. Mia noticed Evie almost glowed with happiness, despite her drama. Roses bloomed on her cheeks and her hair was newly coiffed in a queenlike crown encircling her head.

"Would it be okay, just this once?" Mia asked slyly. "Pig was at the wedding, you know. She is an invited guest."

"You too?" Evie puffed out her cheeks, turning even rosier.

"Just this once, Evie. It is only the banquet hall, after all. Not the actual restaurant." She smiled down at the little pig, wagging her curly tail. "And Pig's an important member of our hospitality team."

Henry grinned, bright smile on his newly shaven face. His neatly pressed shirt and pale linen trousers completed his transformation to an upstanding member of society. "Come on, Evie. Let her stay." He encircled her shoulders with a caressing arm.

"You two!" Evie threw up her hands in disgust, then quickly patted Pig before bustling away. "You'll be the death of me!" She muttered as she went off, "Just trying to keep the place respectable."

"You shaved," Mia commented to Henry. "It looks very nice," she said, as restrained as she possibly could be.

Henry ran his fingers over his smooth cheeks. "Feels odd still. I'll get used to it soon. Didn't want to go to a wedding looking like a bum." His eyes were on Evie's animated figure, discussing the event with George, not as a headwaiter for once, though he'd certainly planned an event to remember. "Figured I need to let go of the past a little so I could have a future." His eyes strayed back to Evie. "Not sure what's next, but I think life might be worth trying again."

"It looks good on you," Mia agreed. "I think you have a fine future coming to you."

He added, a roguish glint in his eye, "Plus, I didn't like how you were counting up the island's bearded men. Made me nervous."

She burst out laughing.

He strolled off after Evie, Pig trotting briskly at his side.

George came up to Mia, Sandy clasped firmly next to him, their arms entwined. Beaming smiles spread across both faces.

"Congratulations, you two," Mia encircled them both in a warm hug. "It was an absolutely beautiful wedding. Sunset on the beach, you can't do any better than that." She grinned at George's blush. "I told you it's about time you got married," she added tartly. "You certainly found the perfect woman for you. There was no way I was going to allow you to let her get away."

George coughed suddenly.

"Thanks, Ms. Mia," Sandy said, a little shyly.

She looked absolutely lovely, Mia thought, and told her so. Her curly hair puffed around her head, with sparkling pearls strung through—it looked like a halo with her smile radiating joy underneath. Her white dress also had pearls dancing around the edges and showed her curvaceous figure to advantage. "You know, you two can change your minds and go anywhere you want in the

Spinel properties. You're both very special people to me, and I want you to have the best honeymoon ever."

George coughed again and smiled down at Sandy. "We might take you up on that, some other time when we feel like exploring the world. Right now, we just want to set up housekeeping together, maybe see some relatives for a good long visit."

"Family is important." Mia nodded at the tiny elderly lady commanding a wheelchair with her erect stance. Her face was unlined, despite her age, and her dark eyes flashed in merriment. "I'm glad your grandmama was able to come to the wedding."

"Only way I was able to get her to see where I worked," George told her. "I've been telling her to visit for years, but she wouldn't leave her town for any reason. But she had to come to my wedding." He grinned and swung Sandy back towards his grandmama, showing off his beautiful bride.

The steel band resonated through the room, and people danced to the music, laughing as they swayed. Mia chuckled as she watched Julie perform a twisting acrobatic move, bending over backwards as she performed a complicated step. Helps to be a yoga teacher, she thought. Elizabeth looked up into a handsome young man's eyes as they moved to the music. The pulsing music made her feet tap, enjoying the sight of George's grandmama being recklessly pushed into the dance by a grinning kid barely tall enough to see over her shoulder. The game elderly lady clapped her hands in time with the beats.

Dancers swirled around the parquet floor, laughing and singing with the music, pausing for breaks amongst the replete buffet tables. Spicy sweet jerk chicken, fish flaked into an aromatic red sauce, creamy grits, rice and peas, and fried chunks of sweet potato filled the main course table. There was a separate table with all types of fruits, with lovely little custard dishes for those who liked their fruit with sweets. Children piled their plates high, returning for seconds of all they liked best.

At the centerpiece of the buffet was the enormous black cake, an elaborate cake made with all kinds of fruits. The raisins, cherries and currants soaked up rum for six months, before being added to the traditional wedding cake, along with copious amounts of cinnamon and allspice. Spicy, dark and rich, it was the perfect cake to celebrate such an important occasion.

The last rays of sunlight filtered through the open doors, streaking the floor in oranges and pinks. Mia slipped outside, walking down to the beach, admiring the flower bouquets framing the sunset. She sighed. It had been a beautiful wedding.

"Nice wedding, huh?" Buck's voice boomed behind her, making her jump.

"You startled me," Mia accused.

"Sorry," Buck said unrepentantly.

"I was just thinking what a lovely wedding it was. George and Sandy make a perfect couple."

"That they do," Buck agreed. "I wish them a lifetime of happiness." There was a trace of a wobble to his voice. He shoved his hands in his pockets and scuffed his shoe across the sand.

"A lifetime," Mia agreed, thinking back to her husband's eyes on her at their wedding, with his whole heart shining in them. "A lifetime of happiness, indeed."

Buck cleared his throat, starting awkwardly, "So Mia, I was wondering..."

"Yes?"

"How'd you know it was Charlie? I mean, the guy calling himself Charlie?" he asked, his face beet red. "I can't figure it out."

"Skip had identified Charlie as the agent assigned to him based on a photo, which later disappeared." She sighed. "Skip wasn't the most observant. One guy with a dark brown beard would look pretty much like any other guy in a beard to him. Amy could have changed the photo before it was sent, of course, but I think she removed it afterwards to prevent anyone from noticing it was a different man than the supposed agent Charlie since it couldn't be found later. All she had to do was make Charlie look like her partner. It wasn't as if Skip would ever get to see her real partner. He'd be dead."

"There was a lot of money involved, you know," Mia said sadly. "Enough to bribe Amy to kill her partner."

"Amy?" Buck started. "Amy killed him? Not Charlie?"

"The group behind the code messages was gaming the market through Skip Wilson's app, Blare. They had to know how much the feds knew. They wanted to keep making money, if they could. The only way they could know what was happening and keep Skip from giving more information to the government was to bribe the agents assigned to him." Mia sighed, thinking of their conversation at the spa. "Amy was imminently bribable."

"But why? How could she kill her partner?" Buck was truly shocked. Team was everything to him. You never let your team down, even if it got you killed.

"They sent a trained killer, the man masquerading as Charlie Smith. His mission was to find out what Skip had told the government and stop any further information from reaching the feds. Then, he was to kill Skip." She shivered, thinking of his icy brown eyes. "He was a cold blooded assassin for hire."

"He approached Amy, bribing her with more money than her wildest dreams," Mia remembered Amy talking about retiring and living rich. She was sure Amy had leaped at the chance. "Amy hired a boat, which was already part of her official assignment, and arrived on it with her actual partner, leaving him to meet Skip and his group, coming by helicopter."

"Amy killed her partner shortly after arrival. My guess is she took him for a walk up the beach to stretch their legs—saying they wouldn't want to approach Skip directly right after arrival—too obvious. Poor man, he went along for a walk, thinking he could trust her." Mia shivered. "She killed him with a blow to the head."

Buck added, considering, "All she would have to do would be point out a seashell or something on the beach. When he leaned down..."

"Yes," Mia agreed with distaste. "It would have been all too easy for her." She coughed, then continued, "She dragged his body to behind the dive shop, leaving it for her assassin partner to move. She could tell him where it was easily enough—they were sharing a room as Mr. and Mrs. Smith."

"With all the bustle of check-in, they must have decided to move it in the early morning."

"They were probably very surprised when I came by and saw the body when Charlie had gone to get his dive tank. The last thing they wanted was Amy's partner to be identified with the body." Mia thought she had walked very close to death that morning. The only reason she was still alive was they hadn't wanted anyone to believe there had been a murder. A missing guest would have set off alarm bells.

Buck gave her a quick, one handed hug, obviously thinking the same thing. Aloud, he mused, "That supposedly old equipment was actually state of the art under a lot of camouflage. Perfect for a quick trip out to the reef to dump a body."

"I wonder whether the original plan was for Skip to just disappear at sea. He's not incredibly stable, as the world knows from Blare—it would be believable for him to just go off somewhere."

Buck nodded, "That seems to have been the plan. I was talking to Albury and he said Skip seemed to have been on the market gaming action a lot more than he said he had. Skip says not, but," He laughed a little, "Glad I'm not the one sorting out that mess."

They walked slowly along the beach a moment, enjoying the beauty of the pink tinged sand and orange sun easing into the water.

"Still, how did you spot it was Charlie? That he wasn't who he said he was?"

Mia laughed. "I knew it was him as soon as Henry told me Charlie had a beard on arrival and Skip confirmed it."

"But how? Lots of men shave off beards."

"Have you seen Henry?" Mia laughed. "Pasty white skin that was covered up by a beard? They don't grow overnight, you know." She shrugged. "If Charlie had had a full beard long enough to grow it and have it on his official photo, then supposedly shave it off the day before, it would have been noticeable where the beard had been. Maybe not as much as Henry's, with his pale skin, but I would have noticed." She forestalled him, "And I certainly would have noticed makeup hiding it too. He wore enough makeup when he was pretending to be drugged. No, Charlie's beard must have been a fake. Then, I realized his signature was different too."

"Surely he would have practiced that?"

"He wasn't planning on passing as the agent for long, just long enough to get the information and kill Skip. Finding the body drew a whole lot of attention to this island he hadn't planned on. The only person who knew the real agent was his partner—and Amy had every reason in the world to back up his cover."

"Hard to believe," Buck said. He ran his hand across his silver grey hair.

"She wasn't a very nice person," Mia said primly, remembering the poor dead man on the beach. "And sometimes there's no chance to do better."

"She got what she deserved for killing her partner," Buck judged. "Anyone who would do that—" They walked along a minute, then turned back toward the lights of the banquet hall. "It's a good thing more people weren't killed. I still can't believe that young idiot wasn't."

"I believe Skip and his mom are having a nice long vacation together in a remote cabin—one with no internet," Mia said. "Hopefully she'll talk him into a more stable lifestyle. One that gets him in less trouble."

"Doubt it," Buck grunted. "Oh well, each to his own."

They neared the music and the dancing, the beating of the steel drums pulsing with the waves. He swung her into his arms and twirled her around in a circle. They danced a few steps along the beach with joy in their steps.

Laughing as they walked up the stairs, Mia said, "It's been a long time since I danced." She smiled up at him, blue eyes bright.

He grabbed two glasses of champagne, handing her one. "Here's to never forgetting how to dance." His gaze was steady on hers, "To life." The crystal clinked together in a chime.

"To life," Mia repeated.

The big room was warm and bubbling with happiness. Couples danced and families chattered, the threads weaving them together strengthened by the wedding ceremony.

George called out in a ringing voice, shepherding his new bride to the center of the big room, "Everyone quiet! Time for the bouquet!"

Mia heard excited whispering behind her, "Ooh, who's gonna be next?"

Sandy scanned the room, looking for someone in particular. Beaming with happiness, she threw the bouquet of roses straight at her target.

Evie caught the white roses with a startled grab. Her cheeks grew red, as she smiled up at Henry.

Ms. Mia Murder Mysteries
Lighthearted and Fun Mysteries with Satisfying Conclusions.

A luxurious private island paradise, with palm trees and white sand beaches, sets the stage for this classic cozy mystery.

A Gilded Age mansion on a secluded Maine island, perched on rocky cliffs overlooking the ocean, sets the scene for a classic murder mystery.

A stolen treasure, a luxury Southwest resort and a glamorous amateur sleuth—join Ms. Mia in a lighthearted murder mystery with a satisfying conclusion.

An Italian villa vacation turns deadly—Ms. Mia unmasks a cunning poisoner in this lighthearted cozy murder mystery.

Ms. Mia joins her childhood friend for a sunny family getaway at a luxurious Veneto villa. But when a family member is poisoned, the idyllic retreat spirals into a maze of secrets and suspicion. Armed with wit, charm, and a glass of prosecco, Ms. Mia dives into the investigation to catch a killer before they strike again—because murder never takes a holiday!

About the Author

Jennifer Branch weaves cozy mysteries with the vibrant flair of her watercolor paintings, inspired by her renown for capturing the Georgia coast. From her Northwest Georgia studio, she pens the Ms. Mia Murder Mysteries series, starring the charming champagne-sipping sleuth Ms. Mia, who solves murders in glamorous resorts. Her debut mystery, *Ms. Mia and Murder at the Grand Island Hotel*, sweeps readers to a Georgia Sea Islands paradise, followed by *Ms. Mia and Murder at Moose Isle Inn*, set on a Maine island.

As a modern impressionist painter, Jennifer infuses her stories with vivid settings, inspired by her artist's eye. When not writing or painting, she roams Georgia's salt marshes, coastal shores, and beyond with her husband, Roger, sons, Edwin and Owen, and dogs, Scout and Sam, finding inspiration in her travels. Visit Branchstudio.com to join her for more Ms. Mia adventures, books, and art!